# She Flew No Flags

Joan B. Manley

Houghton Mifflin Company
Boston 1995

*With love for my daughter*
*Hope Kingma-Rymek*

Copyright © 1995 by Joan B. Manley

All rights reserved. For information about permission to
reproduce selections from this book, write to Permissions,
Houghton Mifflin Company, 215 Park Avenue South,
New York, New York 10003.

*Library of Congress Cataloging-in-Publication Data*

Manley, Joan B.
  She flew no flags/by Joan B. Manley
    p. cm.
  Summary: In early 1944, as the war rages around them, an American
family travels from India to the United States by ship, under blackout
conditions, through the enemy waters of the Indian and Pacific Oceans.
  ISBN 0-395-71130-4
  [1. World War, 1939–1945 — Pacific Ocean — Juvenile fiction.
2. World War, 1939–1945 — Pacific Ocean — Fiction.   3. Voyages and travel —
Fiction.   4. Ships — Fiction.]      I. Title.
PZ7.M31288Sh   1995        94-27623
[Fic] — dc20                CIP
                            AC

Printed in the United States of America

BP   10   9   8   7   6   5   4   3   2   1

*Eh, Baba dudua,*
*Khugh vich a chal,*
*Utheh sona sutura jal.*
*Ulta pulta, ulta pulta,*
*Sir de bal.*

— Punjabi song that Janet sings

Hey, wise old frog,
Go to the well that's near,
Its deep waters so clear.
Head over heels, head over heels,
Tumble in, head first, without fear.

— Translation by JBM

# One

We called her the *U.S.S. You Know Who,* the troopship on which our family voyaged across the Indian and Pacific Oceans in early 1944. Prior to World War II, she had been an Italian steamship, but having been purchased by the U.S. Navy, she was altered and fitted for carrying military personnel and goods. Painted a two-toned gray, the darker area made to look like huge waves rising along her hull, she flew no flags and wore no name.

It was a matter of wartime security. We understood that. A civilian passenger, for instance, might be so foolish as to write: "Dear So-and-So, at last I'm leaving Bombay . . ." and go on to name the ship and its date of departure. The letter could possibly escape the attention of the censors and fall into the hands of the Japanese, who would be waiting with their torpedoes somewhere in the Indian Ocean. Perhaps it had been some such thing that had led, in the winter of 1942, to the sinking of another troopship three days out of Bombay, with no survivors.

We were told simply to be ready to go on a day's notice, and every morning for a full month my father walked to the docks to try to get a clue as to our date of departure. Finally, on the last day of 1943, we got the news: we were leaving tomorrow, New Year's Day!

We knew it would be a long journey to California, but we didn't know it would take nearly six weeks to get there. We knew it would be a dangerous voyage because our ship would be steaming "singly" — the expression used for ships not traveling in convoy — but we did not anticipate the actual times of fear that lay ahead of us. Nor did we expect to be caught up in the secrets of two of our fellow passengers who became our friends.

We were the Baylors, a family of five, who had lived in the Northwest Frontier Province for the past seven years, although much of that time my brothers and I were in boarding school in the Himalayan Mountains. My father, Samuel, a doctor, was forty-three, but with his ruddy complexion and brown curly hair looked a decade younger, whereas my mother, Nellie, at thirty-nine already had completely white hair. White, not gray. She hated it. She had arrived in India a brunette and was leaving it "an old lady," but her beautiful, youthful face belied that description. When her hair had started to turn white, her Indian friends encouraged her to use henna, but in those days women who dyed their hair were believed to be of questionable character. My parents had deep-set blue eyes, high cheekbones, and prominent noses in common — features we three children inherited (except for the stray gene that allowed my elder brother, Kevin, to have a little nose). He was sixteen, with curly blond hair and crooked teeth, and was nearly as tall as Dad, but about thirty pounds lighter. Hugh, twelve, was even skinnier, mainly because he was a picky eater — a source of daily irritation to Mother. He was blond too, but, unlike Kevin's, his hair hung like a limp mop to the tops of his ears. And then there was me, Janet, looking forward to celebrating my tenth birthday later that month at sea. I was the only chubby one in the family, with long, wavy brown hair. And an overbite. Hugh said I had buck teeth, but they weren't quite that bad. But bad enough. Sometimes I would stand at the bathroom mirror with a towel over my nose, and study my eyes, which I thought were very pretty, and wish I could be a harem girl. My desire to cover my nose and mouth, however, did not extend to envying the *bourka* the married Moslem women wore in the territory we'd lived in before coming to Bombay to wait for our ship.

During those weeks of waiting, we'd stayed at the Presbyterian Mission in the heart of the city. Our rooms were in a five-story brick building with an elevator — a new experience for me, as I'd lived in India since I was two and our home in Taxila had been a bungalow with a flat roof where Hugh had kept his rabbit hutches and pigeon coops. Our host and his wife were the Rev. and Mrs. Williamson. She was barely five feet tall and as thin as a wasp, with a sharp tongue, which seems a strange thing to say because she'd had cancer of the throat and spoke through a device that was hidden behind the layers of lace she'd sewn into the necks of her blouses. Her husband was roly-poly and cheerful, with a big belly that jiggled when he laughed. It had shaken most delightfully when, on Christmas Day, he'd sung in his fine, bass voice, "Ooohh-ooohh, tidings of comfort and joy, *com*fort and *joy* . . . !"

We didn't feel particularly comfortable or joyful that season. Mother wasn't well. For the past year she'd suffered from amoebic dysentery, which had responded to none of Dad's treatments, and we were looking forward to new and better medicines for her in the States. Kevin was also feeling weak on his pins, recovering from a cure for the tapeworm he'd acquired in boarding school, where we three kids had been until November. And Hugh had a fever as the result of an ear infection he got when we went swimming at Bombay's Juno Beach. I was feverish too, developing a boil in my left armpit. We joked with Dad that, as the family of a doctor, we were not a very healthy bunch, whereas he, who had been in close contact with every tropical disease known to mankind, was fit and energetic. But I think he worried a lot. I sensed it in the way he clenched his teeth, and during our routine family prayer times he asked God more often than usual to grant us peace of mind and faith in His governing hand in our lives.

Finally, on New Year's Eve, we were given the number of the dock where we were to report the following morning. We left after breakfast, riding the distance together in one horse-drawn *tonga,* our small bags on our laps, with the Rev. Williamson and our two steamer trunks in a second *tonga.* Certain other items of baggage and a number of crates had been delivered for temporary storage in the dock warehouses.

We passed through Bombay's streets which were more crowded and noisy than those that were more familiar to us, in cities such as Lahore and Delhi, for instance. Mother made quiet remarks as we rode along; she was distressed at the sight of the numerous beggars but impressed by the beauty of the children. It seemed to me that in all of her years in India, her first inclination was to comment on the "abject poverty" and the "filth," but then, as though to relieve her soul, her more generous nature and her keen eye for beauty directed her attention past the rags to the human beings they clothed and beyond the garbage in the streets to the jasmine that climbed over the courtyard walls. Dad, on the other hand, whose professional life had centered on the physical suffering of India's people, directed his eyes, as a tourist, upward, admiring the architecture of temples and mosques. Wherever we had traveled as a family, he had made a point of learning about the famous sites or ruins, and in Bombay he pointed out the great Victorian structures. He told us that on seeing the famous Gateway to India for the first time seven years ago, he had been more thrilled than when he first saw the Statue of Liberty or the Arc de Triomphe, causing Mother to sigh and say, "Oh, Samuel, it's only a huge Imperial eye that has never seen anything but the riches to be had for the taking." Only when we'd seen the Taj Mahal by moonlight, two years ago, had I heard her exclaim with appreciation for an edifice that wasn't a Christian place of worship.

In contrast, we three children saw an India that was quite different from the perceptions of our parents. Having had little experience elsewhere, we made fewer judgments, accepting India as it was; whereas our parents tended to think it was necessary to make changes and have people do things their way. We referred to the States as "home," but India was our real home and we felt at home in it. It helped that we spoke Urdu fluently; that and the fact that we were children allowed us to cross barriers that were closed to most adults, who thought of themselves as expatriates and were, in turn, regarded as such.

Now, as our *tonga* made its way toward the shipyard, I suddenly realized this was our last day in India and that we might not ever return. And when Hugh said, "I miss it already," I knew he was thinking the same thing, and I felt that his senses, like mine, were eagerly recording what was most familiar to us. I absorbed the beautiful faces with dark kohl-lined eyes, the ravaged faces with sunken eyes, and the children running alongside us now, clamoring for coins, grasping at our ankles as we faced backward on the tilting *tonga* seat. And now there was the sharp smell of horse manure, now the soft, flowing pastels of saris, and a fat *babu* in a white Nehru suit with a black vest. Cries of babies and beggars and merchants. Curry cooking. The blare of music on a radio in a shop's doorway. The perfume of cut flowers, roses and marigolds. Other reds and oranges, in the fruits, the clothing, the stacked bolts of cotton. Pockets of putrid smells. The shine of brass and copper pots, and sunlight glinting on hanging bundles of glass bangles. The sudden scents of cumin and cloves and hot bread. Hair oil. Urine. Incense.

Kevin was very quiet. In contrast to me, he'd been very unhappy in boarding school, and I wondered if, like Hugh and me, he would miss India. When I asked him, he said, "I don't know. If this war doesn't end soon, I'll be in the Army, and who knows what could happen?"

I hadn't thought of that before! Here I was, looking and smelling with all my might to capture these last moments in my memory, and Kevin was already thinking of his uncertain future. It dampened my spirits to realize this brother's thoughts were so far removed from mine. It widened the gap of our years.

The *tonga* pulled up at a high metal fence where we were met by an armed guard, a tall Sikh with alert coffee-brown eyes, a thick mustache with twisted upturned ends, and a rifle at his side. He was dressed in the uniform of the Indian Army. Other guards stood at intervals both outside and inside the fence. We stepped down from the *tonga*. Just then the second *tonga* with our trunks arrived, and Rev. Williamson descended clumsily from his perch beside the driver.

"Passports!" the guard demanded.

Dad handed him the one on which we five were pictured together. The man examined it and then looked at each of us carefully.

"You must have one passport a person!"

"No one told me that," Dad replied firmly. "We are one family, traveling together."

"But if you are separated, there will be much difficulty," the Sikh said, shaking his head dubiously.

"We will not be separated," Dad replied sternly.

"Let us hope. And this gentleman?"

"A friend. Seeing us off."

"He may proceed no farther. What of luggage?"

"Just these small bags and those two trunks."

The guard whistled up two coolies in red uniforms and official-looking armbands to carry the steamers, telling them, "Customs!" and off they went with the trunks on their heads.

Rev. Williamson gave each of us a warm hug. "God bless!" and "Courage!" he said, and we thanked him for his many kindnesses and left him at the gate.

Dad, who habitually walked as though to perpetual fires, hurried after the coolies to see to the passage through customs and the safe loading of our extra baggage and crates. For a number of minutes his curly head was clearly visible, as the dock was not crowded. It appeared that scarcely more than two hundred of us civilian "Europeans" and Asians would be boarding. (At that time we didn't know there were five hundred Italian Prisoners of War on board; whenever the ship docked, the POWs were kept in close confinement.)

We had not been able to see the ship from the gate, but now we turned a corner, and there it was! It loomed dark and high and huge. And ugly, I thought. I had hoped for at least a flag or two flapping in the breeze.

"No flags," Hugh said, "so the Japs won't know who we are."

"Why doesn't someone paint a big red sun on the sides so they'll leave us alone?" I suggested.

"Then the British would bomb us," Kevin said. He pointed to the forward deck. "Look at the guns!"

"Heaven help us," Mother whispered.

But the sailors who leaned on the rails and waved to us looked wonderfully spiffy in their navy blue uniforms and white caps. That was my first impression of America — all those friendly young men.

We weren't allowed on board for another two hours, but Kevin spotted some bales of jute we could sit on, and we rested there until Dad returned, his face clouded with a fresh worry as he strode toward us.

"We can't all be in the same cabin," he told us soberly. "We've been assigned to one with only four berths. One of us will have to sleep elsewhere. They say there's a bunk available in a cabin with three Chinamen. I'll go there."

"Oh no!" Mother cried.

Kevin said quietly, "I'll go."

"Oh no!" Mother exclaimed again.

"Well, who else, Mother?" Kevin asked wearily.

"Me," said Hugh. "I'm the black sheep anyway."

Usually when he said that, we laughed, because he was the gentlest and most affectionate of us three children, and Kevin and I perceived him to be the most beloved of our parents; whereas Hugh himself resented his position as the middle child. He believed Kevin had special privileges as the elder son and he thought I was lucky to be the only girl in the family. The facts were that Kevin chafed under Dad's injunction that he "be like a father" to us during our months in boarding school, and I felt overly protected, not being able to go anywhere alone.

But now Hugh's self-pitying assertion was ignored in silence as we all looked down at the five little survival kits in blue canvas bags at our feet.

We'd been told each member of the family must have one, in the event we had to go overboard and endure a number of days in an open lifeboat. The contents to be provided by us were: a sweater, an extra pair of long pants or slacks, one change of underwear and socks, a towel, soap, toothbrush and toothpaste, aspirins, and a jar of Pond's cold cream. Once we were on board ship, certain supplements would be added to each bag, such as: salt tablets, chocolate bars, and a light-weight rubber poncho. Each lifeboat itself, we were told, was supplied with canned fruit, canned meat

11

and cheese, and sealed tins of crackers, as well as enough fresh water to support twenty persons for fourteen days.

The very thought of it was daunting enough, but the information Dad had just brought introduced a new terror: What if the member of the family who was separated from the rest of us couldn't get on the same lifeboat?

A stocky man with a sweating red face and red armbands on his blue uniform came to tell us it was time to board.

"Five Baylors, yes," he said, consulting his clipboard. "Four for C23, one for D48. Once you're on board, someone will show you how to find your cabins. Take your small pieces with you. I'll have my crew deliver your big pieces later." He gave Mother and me stern glances. "You ladies have slacks?"

Mother nodded.

"You'll need them. Good luck, Sir," he added, giving Dad a curt nod.

Dad said to us, "Let's take a look at C23 first. Perhaps you and I could share a bunk, Nellie. Or you and Janet. Or maybe we could put the boys together."

We made our way to the cabin on C deck. Because there were no stairs, we had to go down a series of narrow, absolutely vertical metal ladders.

"Oh my goodness!" Mother said as she looked down the first one. She was afraid of heights.

"Don't look, Nellie," Dad said gently. "Watch

Kevin do it. You see? You go down backward. You don't need to look. Just hang on and let your feet guide you." He took her purse and blue bag from her and slipped their straps over his head, but now he was burdened with three items on his back, as well as his heavy black medical bag in one hand and a stuffed leather briefcase in the other.

"Gimme the black bag, Dad," Hugh said. "I can manage it."

"Toss me your briefcase!" Kevin called from the bottom of the ladder.

Mother started down. When she was halfway there, she looked up at me and said with an uncertain little smile, "I see now why he said we'd need slacks, Janet!"

It got darker as we descended into the "bowels" of the ship, as Mother called it. The narrow gangways were illuminated only by an infrequent red bulb, and we saw that the occasional porthole had been sealed and painted over in the same dark gray as the ship itself.

Cabin C23 was an eight-by-ten-foot space, lit by a single dim bulb, and containing nothing but iron bunkbeds on either side and a sink at one end with a small mirrored medicine cabinet above it.

"Doesn't amount to much, does it?" Dad said, with a solicitous glance at Mother.

"I can't possibly stay in here, Sam," Mother said. "There's no air!" She tended to be somewhat claustrophobic.

Now he gave her the same no-more-of-this-nonsense look that he usually reserved for us kids. "They wouldn't put us down here without air, Nell," he snapped, pointing to a vent from which came the faint warm odors of oil and fish and sewage.

"Just take a whiff, Mother," Hugh said. "The fresh-air smells of Bombay!"

I think he was trying to be helpful, but Dad glowered at him.

"There certainly is no room here for a fifth person," Kevin said, bringing us back to the more serious matter at hand.

It was true. One could see at a glance that the bunks were designed for single occupants, and thin ones at that.

Hugh sat on a bottom bunk and tried to bounce a bit, as though testing it for softness. "Comfortable as a coffin!" he pronounced in Donald Duck talk. He could do it perfectly; it always made us laugh. He got away with the most outrageous statements, talking that way. Once he'd even used it to tell Dad to shut up, and was rewarded with a wan smile instead of a smack.

Dad put an arm around Mother. "This too shall pass," he said quietly. That expression, as well as the phrase ". . . in the eternal order of things," formulated part of their code for coping in tough times. That and prayer.

And now, setting his bags on the floor, Dad said, "Let's pray." He closed the door, and we all knelt at the sides of the bottom bunks, as it was our custom to kneel at our chairs at home for evening prayers.

Dad always talked to God in the language of the King James Bible, speaking in a strong assured voice that managed to combine the tones of utmost reverence with those of absolute confidence in a good friend.

"Our dear Lord," he prayed now, "we praise Thy sovereignty on earth, Thy Providence in the history of nations, and Thy knowledge of the depths of each human heart, and so Thou knowest that today we are deeply troubled and seek Thy guidance in the difficult decision we must make. We ask Thy blessing on this coming voyage and a safe reunion with . . ."

There was a knock on the door.

"One minute!" Dad called out. Perhaps the person hadn't heard him, because the door opened, but then it quickly closed again, and Dad concluded his prayer: ". . . reunion with our loved ones. Above all, we ask for Thy presence in these next few weeks of our lives. Grant us Thy peace, we pray. Amen."

We hurried to rise from our knees, and Dad went to open the door.

The sailor who stood there looked acutely embarrassed and scarcely older than Kevin. He had a round, freckled face, greenish eyes with pale orange lashes, and a copper-colored brushcut, most of which was covered by his stiff white cap. His navy blue uniform — from the wide white-trimmed collar down to the bell-bottomed trousers — was impeccably clean and pressed. Stitched to the sleeves halfway above the elbows were three white V-shaped stripes. He held a number of black rubber things in his arms.

"Dr. Baylor? Petty Officer Michael Turner. Sorry to disturb you, Sir. They sent me down with these here lifebelts y'all need to wear from now on."

He gave me a friendly smile. "Got a kid sister just like you, Miss. What's your name?"

"Janet."

"I like that. Well, Janet, if you'd step up here, I'll show y'all how to wear this thing. You right-handed? Okay then, hold up the right arm and stick the head through. There, you see, it hangs from the left shoulder and acrost yer chest, lettin' you keep yer right arm free. Looks like a Safety Squad sash. You ever in the Safety Squad?"

I shook my head. I had no idea what he was talking about. It certainly didn't feel like a sash to me. It was surprisingly heavy. I saw that the double thickness of sturdy rubber was pleated at the sides, and he pointed out a nozzle tucked inside the inner pleat at mid-chest level.

"Always put it on with this thing right about here, but you wouldn't want to blow it up 'til you need to, and *never* 'til you're up top, remember that. Wouldn't want to get stuck down here like a jackrabbit in a gopher hole. Takes about twenty to thirty breaths to inflate it, but you'll probably have time for that while they lower your lifeboat."

"Young man . . ." Dad began on a cautionary note.

"Sorry, Sir, but they told me to tell y'all this stuff. The kids gotta know it too, 'course."

I told him I guessed when the lifebelt was blown up it would be about as big as the innertubes we kids had played with one year when we'd vacationed on Dal Lake in Kashmir.

"Man no! You'd slip right through somethin' big as that. No, this'll fit a whole lot snugger."

Dad said, "I imagine we're to keep these available, along with our kits."

"Oh no, Sir, this you gotta wear night and day. Over your pajamas, even. Not that you got to go to bed with it on or nothin', but you never know when there's gonna be an Alert, so you go to the head in the night and an S.P. catches you without it, you could get put in the slammer. Here we call it the brig." He must have seen some anxiety registered on our faces because he quickly added, "Not to worry, you're safe as houses on this crate. We're well armed to protect ourselves, Sir," he went on with an encouraging nod at Dad, "so you needn't worry none."

"We saw the guns on the front deck," Hugh said. "What kind are they?"

"On the forward deck? We got three- and five-inch 50-caliber guns and . . ."

" 'Inch'?" I echoed in perplexity.

"That's the bore diameter," Petty Officer Turner explained with a grin. "And there's 20mm AA. Antiaircraft, those are. Fore 'n' aft. We try and keep everythin' low-profile much as possible. That plus the paint job and runnin' blackout, it's all part of the disguise." He gave a quiet chuckle. "Heck, you look closely, you'll even see one of the smokestacks is a fake. But we show up on a Jap periscope, I don't guess they'll mistake us for a slow boat to China exactly."

He asked Hugh what his name was. "Well, stick around, Hugh, and you might get to see the guns in action. In *real* action you'll be below decks, but I meant once in a while the captain orders firing practice and they shoot off a few hundred rounds. Got a kid brother, and I know *he'd* love to see it!"

"Yeah, I'd like to see it too, Mr. Turner."

"Call me Mike. From Texas. Where y'all from?"

"Northwest Frontier Province," Hugh said.

"No, I mean *really*."

"Michigan."

"Cold up there," he remarked pleasantly. "Noticed you folks prayin' a while ago. I'm a believer too. Baptist. And you?"

"Presbyterian."

"All the same, ain't it?" Mike looked at his watch. "One more thing. Cap'n wants to see all civilians topside, sixteen hundred hours sharp. Wear your lifebelts. Well, folks, it's been great meetin' you. Oh, almost forgot, put those guardrails up when you bunk. This thing rolls like a pig in a mudbath."

When he was gone, Mother said, "Seems like a nice boy."

"He misses his family, that's for sure," Kevin remarked. "And I think he's lonely. You can see it in his eyes."

"Sixteen hundred hours," Dad said. "That's four o'clock. We must hurry then. I want to meet those Chinese and take a look at their cabin."

D deck was gloomier than C deck, and Number 48 was even narrower than our cabin. The three Chinese persons, dressed in Western clothes, were already there: a small elderly man with kind brown eyes behind wire-rimmed spectacles; a stocky young man who appeared to be in his twenties; and a boy, the most beautiful I'd ever seen — there was no other word for it. Something in his dark eyes told me he was bright, too. I envied him his silky tan skin, his little nose and perfect mouth. But he needed a haircut. His thick black hair with hints of brown in it hung raggedly down to his eyebrows and over his ears. He reminded me of Kipling's Moguli — a Eurasian version. I judged him to be about eight years old. (Later he told me he was ten.) Certainly he was a lot smaller than I was!

Dad introduced us, and the man, Mr. Huang, gave Kevin a little bow and said, "Expecting you, yes. So welcome!"

"We're not sure . . ." Dad began.

"He safe with us, have no fear!" Mr. Huang said, bobbing his head and folding his arms across his chest. "We in boat together, huh?" He gave Kevin an exquisitely tender smile.

Dad said a bit stiffly, "That's not decided yet."

"Forgive me, it is only that officer came to explain us young man best suited here. But it is you to decide, yes."

He waved us into the small space. "Please, to sit!" He looked helplessly around. "Forgive, no chairs!"

Mother and Dad sat hunched on one lower bunk, facing Mr. Huang on the other, while we young people stood squeezed together at either end of the cabin.

"Lee!" Mr. Huang said sharply, adding some words I didn't understand.

So that's the boy's name, I thought as I watched him pass around a Saltines tin filled with what looked like little dumplings. They were won ton, Mr. Huang told us. Stuffed with shrimp. Mother and Dad politely declined, but Kevin, Hugh, and I each took one. It was delicious.

Dad leaned toward the man. "You understand it is difficult for us to have any one member of our family apart from the rest of us."

When Mr. Huang nodded soberly, Dad continued, "Kevin has volunteered to be the one, suggesting it would be wise for me to stay near my wife and the younger children."

"Very wise," Mr. Huang said quietly, nodding again.

"My wife is not altogether well, and, uh, it would make no sense whatsoever for *me* to be here with you and leave the four of them without my support in case . . ."

Dad put his head in his hands a few moments. No one said a word. At length he looked up and said heavily, "I feel terribly guilty, but I simply don't know what else to do."

I glanced at Kevin, expecting him to tell Dad not to worry so much, that it was okay, but Kevin's face betrayed no emotion, and I realized he wasn't going to make it any easier for Dad, because there was a certain core of anger in Kevin that he'd let Hugh and me see from time to time. Once in a bitter moment he'd said, "Dad and Mother love God more than us," but I didn't find that very strange because we'd been told it was *right* to love God first, and I believed it although I couldn't really get a feel for it. But then Kevin said, "Heck, Dad loves *himself* more 'n anyone!" and that surprised me because I, too, loved myself best but felt I ought not to. It shocked me to think our father might feel the same way about himself, since I thought of him, with all his wonderful brains and capabilities, as the most self-sacrificial person I knew! But Kevin said it was just that Dad loved playing the part of a god himself, even if it was on a pretty small stage. "You know he's practically worshiped," Kevin said. "Heck, *I* practically worship him, but he makes me mad, too." So now I felt Kevin was willing to be a martyr but also wasn't minding it that it made Dad feel guilty.

I looked around. Mother was pale. Her lovely aquamarine eyes, riveted on Dad, were filled with empathy for him. One of her slim hands was squeezing the other in her lap. The young Chinese man was staring resolutely at his shoes. Hugh was watching Kevin, and

21

then I noticed the Chinese boy, Lee, was watching me. He gave me a shy smile and quickly looked away. I wondered if he knew how to play jacks.

Mr. Huang was saying in a consoling tone, "A place only, I think, Dr. Baylor, for your son to sleep. He want to be with his family in day."

"Yes, I suppose . . ."

"His clothes are mixed in with ours in the steamers," Mother inserted. She was already thinking of the practical matters connected with Kevin's being separated from us.

"There isn't much, Mother," he spoke up for the first time since we'd entered this cabin. "I'll find a box for the stuff and stick it under the bunk. I'll be fine."

So that decided it. What else, after all, was to be done about the situation?

But other worries occurred to us once we'd had our meeting with Captain Jackson.

We passengers were assembled on the forward deck, and while we stood waiting for the captain to appear, I observed my immediate neighbors. Close by me stood an elderly couple who held hands. The skin of their thin faces was as dry and gray as their hair, the robin's-egg blue of their eyes so pale I imagined India's sun had faded them over the course of many years. The man's frayed white backward collar under his baggy gray suit told me they were missionaries. I liked playing this game, guessing about people, and whenever I found myself in unusual circumstances, such as the present one, it interested me to take note of the strangers about me. I always wondered what had brought them, like me, to this moment. I realized in this case I'd have time to find out someday; I would ask the elderly couple how long they'd been in India and if they'd had any unusual adventures. Near them stood an attractive woman who appeared to be European but wore a dark green cotton sari and had pulled her long honey-colored hair back in a single braid. She seemed tense and preoccupied. I imagined she had come to India alone, married an Indian, and was leaving him now. Why? That was a question I would hardly dare ask, and if I ever did, she probably wouldn't tell me, and if she did, her answer would no doubt be quite different from the story I'd made up, as was often the case when I had the chance to find out if my guess was right or not. Near her stood a darkly tanned man who was smoking a cigar and rested his left hand on the hilt of an unsheathed *kukri* thrust under the wide belt of his jungle jacket. He was the former manager of a rubber plantation in Burma, I told myself, and when the Japanese took over, he hid in a hut and eventually made his way through a jungly patch, cutting through the underbrush with that sharp curved knife until he reached a railway and hopped a train into India. Looking at his stern, closed face, I doubted I would ever be able to find out who he really was. He appeared to be acquainted with the man who stood beside him, a man more emaciated than any I'd ever seen, and I had seen many on India's streets. His eyes were sunk deep in their sockets and his skin was as darkly yellow as an old lemon.

I whispered to Dad, "What's wrong with him?"

Dad put his mouth to my ear. "Liver damage. Hepatitis, perhaps. Or too many bouts of malaria and too much atabrine. Don't stare at him."

"I'm not!"

I looked up at the European woman in the sari, wondering if she had overheard us, but her attention was directed elsewhere. I followed the line of her intent gaze and saw she was looking at Lee, the Eurasian boy.

Yes, I thought with a twinge of envy, he is that beautiful, people would look at him.

As I was wondering if there were any other children on board, people's heads turned to watch the captain descend from the bridge and stand behind a railing from which he could see us and address his remarks. He was a man of average height, with chipmunk cheeks and the hint of a pot belly. Against the navy blue of his officer's uniform, the gold star and the four wide gold stripes showed up nicely at the ends of the sleeves. Over the left vest pocket were rows of colorful decorations, and I wondered what he had done to receive the honors. On the visor of his cap was a pattern of something that looked like golden pinecones.

"Good afternoon. I'm Captain Jackson. Welcome aboard," he began in a voice that rang with authority. "As you can see, this is no pleasure liner, but my crew and I will do what we can to make you as comfortable as possible, providing you keep your requests to a minimum." Now he gave us a warm smile. "Seaman Cooper is passing out a booklet of schedules and regulations I urge you to study. It was produced, by the way, on our own printing press. For those of you who can't live without a daily newspaper, we publish one, such as it is, and you're welcome to contribute to it. Anecdotes are appreciated; opinions are censored."

He smiled again at his own joke and continued on a more serious note, "Let me call your attention to the fact that both our civilian mess and lounge are too small to accommodate all of you at one time. Kindly keep to the C- and D-deck schedules."

At this, Dad leaned across to Kevin and whispered, "I'll talk to him about that. We want you with us!"

The captain went on, "I hope you'll understand that you are allotted limited deck space. And your promenade times are scheduled for only certain after-dark hours. I would advise you to take advantage of the time you'll have for afternoon naps."

He paused to look us over, his eyes registering concern when they paused here and there on certain individuals, such as the old man and his wife next to me. And then on me! I smiled to reassure him he had nothing to worry about.

The captain continued forcefully: "You will have noticed the portholes are sealed and painted. We will be running under FULL BLACKOUT conditions. And maintaining radio silence. In addition, all of the ship's waste products — garbage and that sort of thing — are discarded after dark, to allow it to sink by morning. You must NEVER throw anything overboard. No papers, for instance. Not even a cigarette butt."

He looked here and there in the audience and said sternly, "By the way, those of you who smoke may do so ONLY in the lounge, where one of our Shore Patrol men will be posted to look after you. A fire on board is always serious, but, more seriously, its smoke can be seen at great distances, which constitutes a hazard to us all. NEVER smoke on deck! At sea, a lighted match or glowing cigarette end can be seen two miles away at night. A civilian who commits such an offense will be treated according to ship's rules, which is to say, he or she will complete the journey in the brig."

Mother and Dad exchanged pleased glances. They were not fond of smokers.

"If a fire should break out," Captain Jackson went on authoritatively, "the Alert will sound, which will mean that, wherever you are, you must return to your cabin with all possible speed and prepare to abandon ship, in the unlikely event it should come to that."

I was standing next to Mother, and she reached for my hand and held it in both of hers.

"Be aware that this particular ship was originally equipped with fire walls, a feature the Navy left in place. The walls partition the ship's six hundred fifty-two feet in three sections. Should you find yourself in a section not your own, find temporary asylum in someone else's cabin. But, in the event the Abandon Ship alarm should sound, you MUST go to your own lifeboat, and hence the stipulation that you wear your lifebelt at all times outside your cabin. You will be acquainted with the lifeboats later."

Now all five of us looked at one another, realizing our worst fear — that Kevin would be assigned to a different lifeboat than ours — and once again Dad whispered to Kevin, "I'll talk to him about that, too!"

Captain Jackson touched his visor and gave us a nod. "The next thing on the agenda is to acquaint you with the sounds of the alarms. I'm, of course, anticipating a smooth and uneventful voyage. I ask only for your patience and cooperation. The rest you can leave to us. Are there any questions?"

The American-sounding voice of a woman at the rear asked, "What time will we set sail?"

"At an undisclosed hour, Madam."

"I just wondered if I'd have time to run ashore for one last batch of *samosas,*" she said, referring to the delectable Indian pastries stuffed with curried potatoes and peas.

"Bring some for me!" a rich Scots voice called out.

Everyone laughed.

Captain Jackson smiled. "There may be time for that, yes, but I would advise against it, given the diligence of the guards at the gate."

"Oh, they'd understand, mate!" the same Scots voice

rang out, and again the group responded appreciatively.

"Kindly stay put, Madam," the captain said, "and save your appetite for the fine dinner our chef has prepared for you. Any other questions?"

Dad raised his hand. "I noticed the hull is riding high above its waterline. May I know what's in the hold?"

Captain Jackson looked sternly down at him. "You may not!" But then he squinted and regarded him for a long moment. "Dr. Baylor, is it?"

"Yes."

"I'd like a word with you, Doctor, in my quarters, as soon as this assembly is concluded."

My first reaction to this interchange was one of fear. It had been a bold question, sharply rebuked, and now Dad was in trouble, I thought. But then I realized the captain somehow already knew of Dad's identity and had taken particular notice of his presence on board, and that gave me a sense of relief. I felt proud, too, the same kind of pride I'd felt when once, in a church in Rawalpindi, a British soldier had collapsed during the service, and an officer had barked, "Is there a doctor here?" and Dad had said, "Yes, here!" The man had had a cardiac arrest, and Dad had pounded on his chest to make his heart beat again, and revived him.

"Dr. Baylor!" It was the man in the collar who stood near me. "James Foster," he said, extending his hand. "I met you at an interdenominational conference in

Delhi, four years ago. My wife and I are friends of your friends, the McPhersons."

"But of course!" Dad said, shaking his hand warmly. "I remember you!" and I could see that he did. Among the millions of people on the huge subcontinent of India, fellow missionaries tended to recognize one another or knew friends who knew friends, flocking together like migratory barn swallows with long tails among indigenous herons with long legs. Mother had never met Mrs. Foster, but as they greeted each other, I sensed each of them had found a friend, at least for the duration of this voyage. I was glad for Mother because I knew that for much of our seven years in India she had been lonely, with Dad keeping long hours at the hospital, we kids gone for nine months of the year, and her nearest friend, Jackie Downing, stationed in Rawalpindi — not more than thirty miles away, but petrol was rationed, so they seldom saw each other.

I heard her tell the woman, "I'm terribly worried about our son, Kevin, who has to be apart from us, on D deck. What if . . . ?"

". . . talk with the captain about that now," Dad was saying to the man. "I appreciate your concern, Reverend Foster."

We were next introduced to the alarms and were told it would be highly unlikely the Abandon Ship alarm would sound before we'd had warning from one of the others. There was the Alert, for instance, an insistent BEH–BEH–BEH–BEH, which meant "All

Hands on Deck," while all others — civilian passengers as well as troop-class passengers — had to return to or remain in their cabins, with lifebelts on and survival kits in hand until further notice. It would be sounded in the event of any emergency, including a fire on board. The General Quarters alarm was a piercing KOO–EEE–YOO! like a giant prehistoric bird in pain, followed by the sound of fierce, urgent bells. It meant "Man Your Battle Stations" and everyone else sit tight until such time as a sighted vessel had been identified. The Abandon Ship alarm itself was more familiar, a siren that reminded me of the practice bomb alerts in Taxila, when we had had to run to the underground shelter we'd been told to construct near our house; but a true alert never came, so Hugh and I played in there with the village kids. Were we to hear that sound, we should proceed with all possible haste to our lifeboats. Later tonight, they wouldn't say when, we would be subjected to a disaster drill.

"Oh dear, we'll have to race up those ladders like rats, Sam," I overheard Mother say quietly to Dad. "What if I'm . . . indisposed just then? What if I'm in the . . . What did that Turner boy call it? 'The head.' What a strange word for it!"

"Nellie, it's not likely to happen," he replied soothingly, "but if it does, I think you'll find one urgency superseding the other."

He had said the last part lightly, but I could see Mother was still troubled by the thought of an emergency and being caught in the bathroom where she spent a good deal of time because of her illness.

"You'll wait for me, won't you?" she asked in a voice so like a little girl's I suddenly saw her as she must have been in her youth, feeling scared and vulnerable once in a while and needing someone older to depend on. It was a strange thing to think that she sometimes needed Dad the way I needed her. It was Mother to whom I went with my problems and missed the more keenly when I was away at school; whereas I thought of Dad as the solver of truly big problems, the kind that involved the whole family, such as what to do when there was an earthquake or our luggage was lost or our road in the mountains was blocked by a landslide. At times like that we all looked to him, and I wondered now if he ever felt small himself. It seemed to me that when he clenched his teeth or prayed or put his head in his hands, as he'd done in the Chinese cabin, he was worrying about us, yes, but did *he* ever really *need* anyone? And as I thought these things, with Mother's little-girl voice still in my heart, I watched my father put an arm around her shoulders and draw her to him in a rare public display of emotion.

"Oh, my dear!" he said softly. " 'Til death do us part!"

Before the assembly was dismissed, we all listened to the final sound, the All Clear, an ear-splitting but somehow cheerfully rising HOOOOOT! HOOOOOT! HOOOOOT! HOOT!

Finally, we were reminded to consult the booklet

we'd been given, in which the most direct routes from cabins to lifeboats were outlined, and in preparation for the later rehearsal Dad took a look at it before going to his meeting with the captain.

"It's just as we feared," he said grimly. "Kevin's lifeboat is Number Two, starboard, ours is Number Four, port. I suspect Captain Jackson will tell me that to insist on Kevin's joining us will only serve to put him in further jeopardy, in the event . . . Well, I must go now. Wait for me before going to D deck."

"Come, children," Mother said, "let's see if our trunks have been delivered."

That was the sort of thing she took calm control of, and we soon had Kevin's clothing and toiletries sorted out and the four bunks neatly made.

I wanted a top bunk. Climbing up there would remind me a bit of the treehouse my brothers had built in a pepper tree at home in Taxila. The three of us had consumed a number of jars of homemade peanut butter up there, and sometimes I'd enjoyed hours of privacy in the treehouse, reading the books the school library let me take home for the months of vacation. Those were the best times, being alone with a good book, while Kevin was working on his art in his room and Hugh was on the roof with his pigeons or was working on his bug and stamp collections. But now of course Hugh wanted a top bunk, too, and Mother had to put an end to our quarrel by deciding that she and I should have the lower bunks. She often had to get up during the night, she said. I understood that, but I couldn't see what that had to do with *me*. Just because *she* . . . It was things like that which sometimes made me resent being a girl.

Dad returned from his visit with the captain. He'd received permission for Kevin to take his meals with us and spend his reading room and deck hours at the same time we did, but, no, a reassignment of lifeboats was out of the question, for precisely the reason Dad had surmised.

"Captain Jackson says we should put our fears over this lifeboat business out of our minds," Dad told us, "because nothing of the sort is likely to happen."

"But they're still going to make us go through the routine, I'll bet," Kevin said sullenly.

"Like fire drills at school, Kevin," Dad replied with an impatient edge to his voice. "Now, I suggest we all take the captain's advice."

"And trust in the Lord," Mother added.

"Which lifeboat is *He* going to get on?" Kevin asked, his crooked teeth showing in a smile that didn't match the troubled look in his eyes.

Dad sighed. "You know very well . . ." he began, but Hugh interrupted to ask why the captain had wanted to talk with Dad in the first place.

"I can't tell you that part."

"Why not?"

"Military secret."

"But you can tell *us!*"

"No, I've given my word not to talk about it. But you'll know in time."

Kevin said, "Obviously it's got something to do with the hold. He didn't like your question about that. Maybe this ship ran arms and tanks and other stuff to the Pacific war zone and is going back empty, so we're riding high in the water, like you said, Dad. But why should that be a secret?"

There was a responsive glint in Dad's eyes, but no further coaxing could get another word about it out of him, and we soon gave up, because, as a doctor, he'd had lots of practice at keeping secrets.

Not long thereafter, through a little speaker in the wall came the sound of a mellow male voice saying, "All passengers on C deck, this is your chef, inviting you to dinner, pronto." We heard a distant snort of laughter, then the chef's voice again. "Meal calls from now on, folks, will sound like this." There was a sharp click, followed by a soft DING–DING–DING.

Dad chuckled. "That seems to be the one feature of this old steamship they left intact from the old days, eh, Nellie?"

"Yeah, I remember now, too," Kevin said, who'd been almost my age when our family had voyaged to India by way of the Atlantic, the Mediterranean, and the Red Sea. "There was a guy who played the bagpipes every night, wasn't there? And I remember games on deck." He turned to me. "You won the potato race for the two-year-olds, Jannie."

34

"And she's been racing to the potatoes ever since," Hugh said, punching my arm, the one with the boil in the armpit, which hurt so much I had to give him a really solid punch back.

"That's enough!" Mother said. "Brush your hair, Janet. Tuck your shirt in, Hugh. Let's go see what this dinner's like."

We climbed two ladders to the dining room, which the captain had called the civilian mess — a misnomer, I thought, because it was marvelously neat and shiny, with comfortable chairs around various-sized tables that were bolted to the floor, and vases, even, with fresh marigolds in them.

The old couple we'd met, the Rev. and Mrs. Foster, were already eating at a small table in one corner. They were having an animated discussion and seemed to be enjoying each other, whereas the European woman, sitting alone at a nearby table, was reading a book while she picked at her food. She had changed into a pale blue silk sari with gold-stitched borders and, in spite of the obligatory lifebelt, looked elegant. But unhappy.

The dinner was beyond all expectation or imagining — my first encounter with America's plenty, even though it was wartime. It was served cafeteria style, a new phenomenon to me, and Mother cautioned me about my eyes being bigger than my stomach. I had to choose, for instance, between ham or fried chicken, sweet or mashed potatoes, green beans or corn, pickles or sliced beets, butter or gravy, muffins or corn bread, and not being able to make such crucial decisions on the spot, with this feast laid before me, I took a portion of everything, and I guess Mother let me do it to teach me a lesson.

I picked up my fork, eager to dig in.

Dad frowned. "We haven't said grace yet."

"Oh Dad . . ." I muttered. I didn't like praying in public places. Furthermore, I thought that even in the privacy of our home we prayed altogether too often: before and after meals, at evening Bible reading and prayer time, and again at bedtime. If God knew what was in our hearts, why did we have to *say* it, I wondered.

"You don't begrudge God a little thanks, do you, Janet? Let's bow our heads for a few moments and say a silent prayer."

I closed my eyes for the second it took to think Thanks and went straight to my sweet potatoes.

"My, I haven't had such tender chicken in years," Mother said. "And such lovely corn!"

Kevin said, "These pickles are like when I was a kid."

We all agreed, everything tasted wonderful. But I'd taken too much. It bothered me to let so much of my selections go to waste.

"Will you keep it for me?" I asked the steward who came to pick up our trays.

"What doesn't get eaten, gets dumped."

"But all this ham . . . !"

"Tomorrow it's hot dogs, spaghetti, stuff like that.

You like hot dogs, don't you?"

I nodded dubiously. I'd never had one.

"You can go for dessert now," he said with a grin. "There's ice cream, pie, and cake. And Jell-O."

"What's that last thing?"

"You don't know Jell-O? Where you been, anyway?"

Dad, who had a notorious sweet tooth, returned to the table with three desserts for himself.

"I won't do this every day, Nellie, I promise. But just look at what they had to offer!"

He had selected apple pie with vanilla ice cream on it, a chocolate drink he called a malted, and a bowl of shiny red stuff that quivered when he touched it.

"Want some?" he asked. "Tastes like strawberries," but I shook my head. I was too full. I resolved to try just one new treat a day from now on.

As though he'd read my mind, Hugh said, "Good for you." He ate a spoonful of ice cream with nuts in it. "You don't want to look like a blimp by the time we get to Michigan."

Sometimes I hated him.

When the same steward came for the dessert trays, Mother asked him where we could find a carton for Kevin's clothing, and the young man brought us an orange crate. We returned to C23, packed Kevin's things, and went to D48.

Dad knocked, and Lee came to the door. He was barefoot, wore red and yellow print pajamas, and looked more beautiful than ever, I thought. It wasn't fair.

His eyes went first to me, but then he said to Kevin, "Uncle said you would come. He said I should wait."

"But what about your supper?" Mother asked.

Lee laid a hand on his stomach and gave a mock grimace. "Too much won ton."

I saw he had wrapped his lifebelt around his waist, folding it to take up the slack and securing it with a huge safety pin that looked as if it had once been on a kilt.

"You've put holes in it," I said. "The air will come out."

He shrugged. "Not before the sharks eat me."

"Sharks!" I hadn't thought of that. "But we'll be in boats!"

"Then why do we need belts?"

I thought for a second. "In case the boat tips over."

"Yes, that's when the sharks come."

Dad put up a cautionary hand. "Enough now, children. It's not always healthy to let your imagination run away with you."

"Got my stuff here," Kevin said to Lee. "Where should I put it?"

"Under there. You and Uncle have the bottom bunks, okay?"

The "okay" surprised me, and I wondered where he'd gone to school. And where were his parents?

"Is the other man your brother?" I asked. "What's his name?"

"Dao-Zeun. No relation. He's just traveling with us. His parents were killed by the Japanese. Chopped their heads off."

I wanted to hear more, but Mother said, "How awful!" and laid a hand on my arm, which was a signal not to get too personal with my questions.

"What's your name?" Lee asked me.

I told him, and immediately he asked, "Janet, you play checkers?"

"Sure, anyone can play checkers."

"How about chess?"

"I don't know chess."

"Not everyone can play chess."

Hoping to stump him, I asked, "Can you play jacks?"

"Of course! But that's a girl's game."

"It doesn't have to be," I snapped. "Hugh plays with me sometimes."

"Okay, then, I'll play you sometime."

We smiled at each other, and I felt that, like Mother's meeting Mrs. Foster, I, too, had already found a friend and things were looking up. I had Hugh to be with, too, of course, but often he would go off exploring by himself or would spend hours poring over his biology books, and other times I'd noticed he liked my company mainly when we were doing something *he* wanted to do and wasn't so eager when it was something *I'd* chosen. Being a boy, Lee might turn out the same way, I thought, but he was smaller than me, so maybe I could show him a thing or two.

"Dad," I asked, "do you think Lee could be with us when Kevin is?"

"Well, I don't know . . ." Dad began cautiously. "He'll want to stay with his uncle, I should think, won't he? Won't you?" he asked Lee.

Before Lee had a chance to answer, I told him excitedly, "Kevin gets to be with us for meals and other times."

"I would like very much to be with the people of C deck," Lee replied shyly.

It seemed a very formal and roundabout answer. Why hadn't he just said he would like to be with us? With me?

Mother said coolly, "We'll have to discuss it, Janet."

When we were back in our cabin, having hugged Kevin "So long!" and "Be brave!" she scolded, "That question about Lee being with us was awkward. That was something you should have asked us about first. Those times will be our special times with Kevin. Our family times together. I'm not at all sure I like the idea of that boy eating with us all the time. We don't know anything about him, really," which I took to mean, knowing Mother, that she suspected he wasn't a Christian, and now I regretted having suggested he join us. I would be embarrassed to have him watch us pray three times a day.

# Two

We were getting ready for bed when the first of the alarms went off, the BEH–BEH–BEH–BEH somewhat muffled now as it came through the speaker.

"At least they didn't wait until we were asleep," Mother said. "Let's hurry and get into our slacks, Janet."

The sound went on and on.

Mother went to the mirror to brush her hair and powder her nose.

"We're not going to a party, Mother," Hugh teased.

"Habit, I guess."

We got out our survival kits and checked their contents again, as though a thief might have come in while we were out and stolen something.

"Where's your third Hershey bar, Jannie?" Hugh asked. "I'll bet you've already eaten it!"

I nodded reluctantly. "We didn't have lunch. I got hungry."

"You had five pancakes for breakfast, for pete's sake!"

"Leave me alone."

"You eat the other two, don't expect to share mine!"

"I'd rather starve."

The General Quarters alarm sounded. More Standby for us. We had to wait for the Abandon Ship siren. When it finally came, I felt the small hairs lift on the back of my neck.

"Here we go," Dad said calmly. "Remember kids, Nellie, this is only a practice."

The narrow gangway was crowded but strangely quiet, except for the sound of the siren, as people with desperate looks on their faces pressed toward the first ladder where a Shore Patrol man stood on guard. He held a nightstick. His pistol rested in its black holster on his hip. One woman pushed another aside in her eagerness to scramble up the ladder.

"Take it easy, lady!" the S.P. said sharply. "All right, one at a time now! Move it along! Hey, you! Women and children first!"

"Since when?"

"Rule of the sea, buddy! All of you men, step aside and let the women and children go up first!"

"I'll stay behind with you, Sam," Mother said.

"No, you won't," Dad replied firmly. "Go with the kids. Hugh, look after your mother and sister."

"I'm not a child, Sam," Mother retorted, her eyes narrowing with resentment.

"No, of course not. You'll look after each other. I'll

meet you up top. Go on now. Remember, boat four, port side."

"What side is that?"

"Come on, Mother," Hugh said, taking her hand, "I know where that is."

"You!" the S.P. barked. "You heard me!" and I saw he was pointing his billy club at another of the persons I'd noticed during the assembly — the man I had imagined was a former manager of a rubber plantation. He had his arm around the bony man with old-lemon skin, who looked like he was about to faint.

"Rules be damned, mate, this man's sick!" the man shouted above the wail of the siren.

"I can see that," the S.P. said quickly. "Take him back to his cabin. He doesn't need to go through this. I suggest you get in touch with the Chief Medical Officer, Sir."

As we made our way through the maze of gangways and up three double sets of ladders, the people around us got noisier and pushier. Some men paid no attention to the "Rule of the sea," and all along the line they were sharply rebuked by the S.P.s that were stationed at various points to keep order. It worried me what it might be like if this weren't just a practice run, or a drill, as they'd called it. Certainly it was no *run*. Clots of shoving people formed at the base of each ladder, and certain individuals, once it was their turn, tended to wait until the person ahead of them was all the way up. And some people Mother's age and older behaved as though they'd never seen a ladder before, bringing the second foot up next to the first and looking down before they stepped up to the next metal rung, as though they expected it to be missing.

"Go up it like stairs, Mother," I said impatiently, my nose at the back of her knees. "You don't have to look!"

"Come on, Mother," Hugh encouraged her from the top of the ladder.

"This is hard on my heart," she gasped. "I can't catch my breath."

"You're just hyperventilating," Hugh said. (He liked using Dad's medical terms.) "Come on, you can make it!"

At length we pushed open the last heavy door and emerged onto the deck and into the night air, which was cool now. It smelled of fuel oil, with hints of dead fish and rotting seaweed.

It seemed strange to find the ship as peacefully docked as it had been when we'd boarded hours ago. Under the shaded yellow lights on the dock below, antlike columns of red-coated porters with loads on their heads were advancing at a swift pace toward the ship and up the gangplank. Beyond the roofs of the warehouses the bustling city of Bombay was dark and quiet now, given the rules of blackout and curfew — only cooking fires glowing softly here and there and an occasional orange light of an unshuttered window winking. Over the city hung a shred of the old moon.

On deck the sailors worked at the winches that swung the lifeboats out from their moorings until they hung clear of the ship's sides and swayed gently, high above the black water.

The siren was abruptly turned off, the HOOOOOT! of the All Clear sounded briefly, and someone on a bull-horn informed us that this was as far as it went for to-night, folks. The boats, he explained, neither couldn't nor wouldn't be lowered unless the ship was clear of the port. As for our getting into them, yes, good question, he said. See the rope ladders and the nets? Yes, those bundles attached to the edge. Well, when necessary, they would be tossed over, and we would climb down them and then get into the boats. Not to panic. Jump overboard only in the worst of emergencies, because it was much harder to get into a boat up from out of the water than down from a ladder. And here, too, yes, it was always the women and children who went first, let's us gentlemen remember that, right?

Hugh whispered to me, "There's not nearly enough boats for everyone. But don't tell Mother. She'll worry."

"There's gotta be!" I said aloud.

"Shh! We'll ask Mike about it."

Dad touched my shoulder and put an arm around Mother. "Sam, where've you *been*!" she asked in a harsh whisper, and I saw now how sick with worry she looked. "Did you only just *now* make it up here?"

"I went to see about that jaundiced man."

"For heaven's sake — "

"He's desperately ill."

"Then let him see the *ship's* doctor!"

The man on the bullhorn told us we were free to enjoy the night air as long as we liked. Assembly dismissed.

Hugh and I went to look for Kevin. We spotted him right away, looking for us.

"What a lot of hooey!" he said immediately. "That guy made it sound like the boats would be down there waiting like a bunch of parked taxis. I remember our last trip. Half the time you couldn't even *walk* on the deck, much less go down a rope ladder!"

"That was different," Hugh said. "The Pacific is supposed to be calmer than the Atlantic and the Mediterranean."

"We'll see. Remember what we heard about Jimmy?"

Jimmy was a cousin who had died the previous year. Aunt Edith had written us all about it.

"Jimmy *jumped*," Kevin said.

"No, he didn't," Hugh said. "His buddy said he ran back inside for his life jacket. Jimmy couldn't swim, remember?"

Kevin sighed. "That's right, he ran to get his life jacket. I'd forgotten that part. Anyway, it doesn't make any difference. It was in the North Sea. In December."

"But his buddy got to a lifeboat and lived to tell about it," Hugh insisted.

"Twenty-six of 'em," I inserted, remembering our aunt's letter.

"Picked up by the same German sub that did 'em in," Hugh added. "I like that part. Angels in disguise!"

"Oh, Hugh," Kevin said wearily, "you sound just like Dad. He prays all the time for God to look after us, as though we were special somehow, but . . ."

"We are! He'll look after us! Look how He looked after that friend of Jimmy's!"

"But what about Jimmy? I'll bet he was praying 'Help me!' with all his might, too. There must be millions of people who ask the same thing every day and don't get a special answer."

"Maybe 'cuz it's their time to go," Hugh said, lifting his chin, his expression intent with speculation.

"That's what I mean," Kevin said evenly. "You can't ever assume your time's not up."

"Oh, *I* do!" Hugh replied. "Maybe later, when we get to the States, a bad driver will run me over, but while we're on this ship you won't catch me without my lifebelt, in the first place, and I know how to swim. Heck, I could swim to China if I had to."

"Unless the sharks get you first," I put in.

"But they wouldn't, you see!" he said with a broad grin.

"Why not?"

"Because I know I wasn't born just to be shark food! I *know* that! I'd say to them, like Daniel in the lion's

47

den, 'Sharks, you don't want to eat me. I won't even taste good!' and they would leave me alone."

Kevin turned away and gripped the railing. But then he turned back to Hugh and ruffled his hair. "You're right," he said gently, "you're definitely not cut out to be shark food."

Mother and Dad approached, walking arm-in-arm.

"Here you are!" Mother said. She looked radiant.

"We've been walking together," Dad said. "I've estimated that approximately fifty times up and down the deck space we're allowed equals a mile."

"Isn't it lovely tonight!" Mother said. "Just look at the stars!"

"Our last night in India," Hugh said, his voice heavy with regret.

Later that night, when I'd been asleep a long time, it seemed, the ship's engines started up. Our cabin rumbled and vibrated with the noise.

I heard Mother and then Dad roll over in their bunks. Hugh wasn't stirring, so I asked as quietly as I could over the sound of the engines, "Is it always going to be this noisy?"

"You'll get used to it," Dad replied. "Go back to sleep now."

"I can't!"

"Well, just lie quietly."

"I don't need these covers on."

"Kick them off, then. Good night, Janet."

I lay awake, listening to clankings and bangings going on in different parts of the ship, and doubted I'd ever sleep again. I missed the distant sounds of Taxila's jackals and the crunching of the mission guard's boots on gravel as he walked up and down outside our bungalow. And I missed the night sounds in the mountains — owls calling and the pines whispering in the wind and the roar of rain on the roof.

The pitch of the engines changed, and I sensed the ship was beginning to move, but it was a long while before I felt the first bit of rolling from side to side.

Dad was snoring. Mother was too, just a little. I wondered if Kevin was asleep also, there in the cabin on D deck with his three Chinese companions. I felt lonely to be the only one awake.

Hugh stirred and a second later his upside-down face hung over the edge of his bunk. I gave him a little wave, and then there he was, coming soundlessly down his little ladder. He had his lifebelt on over his pajamas. I grabbed mine and got up. We didn't say a word to each other; we didn't need to. I knew where he wanted to go, and I wanted to be with him. If Mother, the lighter sleeper, awoke and asked what we were up to, we would say we needed to go to the head. But she didn't awaken. Barefoot and as quiet as snails, taking great care to unlock the door without the slightest click, Hugh and I left the cabin.

When we were a number of feet away from the door, Hugh put a Stop-now hand on my shoulder. I could barely see his face in the darkness of our little corridor, which intersected with the dim red-lit gangway ahead, but I felt the tension of his excitement over this forbidden adventure. Except for the throb of the engines, it was quiet on C deck, with no one stirring.

He put his mouth to my ear. "There'll be an S.P. under the light at the end, but the bathroom's around the corner from him, and there's a ladder to the next deck beyond that, I noticed, so we'll go up that way."

"There'll be another S.P. up *there!*" I whispered back.

"Same station, same thing. No one knows us yet, Jannie. No one knows where we belong. Put your lifebelt on properly. Okay, let's go. And don't look so scared."

The first S.P. seemed to be practically asleep on his feet. He opened his eyes. "Hi, kids. Up pretty late, aren't you?"

"Diarrhea," Hugh said. "Too much curry."

We rounded the corner. "That will give us a few minutes," Hugh said with a grin.

As Dad had always done before we made our family trips, Hugh had obviously scouted the territory ahead of time, because it worked just as he'd said it would. We got to the forward deck without being challenged.

Oh, the ocean — the Arabian Sea! It was all around us now, swelling darkly under the pale light of the stars and the sliver of the moon. The big guns, their long barrels pointing straight ahead, looked spooky in the gloom.

Hugh gripped my hand. "Let's go stand right up front!"

I delighted in the coolness of the vibrating deck under my bare feet, the mystery of the creakings and groanings of this, our new world, this ship, and the huge sky above us.

We stood at the bow's railing and looked down at the prow thrusting through the water. It was scary to feel the ship dip and to see the water rise up to meet us, coming to within a few feet of our noses, it seemed, before we were lifted up again, leaving the dark water far below and bringing the stars suddenly closer. We watched the water boil whitely away from the ship's sides. There were microscopic plants and sea creatures in it, Hugh said, that accounted for that phosphorescent glow.

"Pretty, huh?" he said. "And look out there! There's India!" He pointed to the black land mass that rose above the inky line of the horizon. It looked like camels lying down in the desert.

"Goodbye, India!" he called. "I'll be back, wait and see!"

"You really wanna come back?" I asked.

"I love it, you know."

"You *hated* school! You hated Ridge Point as much as Kevin did!"

"Ridge Point wasn't really India, Jannie. Anyway, I'm gonna come back as a biologist someday and be a *teacher* there, not a *kid,* and do the things I want to do."

"I want to come with you," I said.

"Sure, we'll come back to India together. There isn't any girl in the world I'd rather go places with."

I felt the same way. I couldn't imagine I would find a boy I would ever love better than I did Hugh at that moment.

Hugh gripped my arm. "Uh-oh, here comes someone!"

Out of the darkness loomed a tall figure in the slate-gray working uniform and the visored cap of an officer.

"What on earth are you kids doing here?" he asked sternly.

"Just lookin'," Hugh said.

"You know it's two in the morning?"

Neither of us answered.

"You can't be up here," the man said. "It's dangerous. It can get pretty rough. You could get swept overboard. And this ship won't stop to pick up anybody, you hear? Nobody!" he added gruffly.

"We can swim," Hugh told him.

"I see. All the way back to India, huh? How'd you get up here anyway? Where are you supposed to be?"

"They're supposed to be with me, Officer," came our father's voice as he approached, his arms pumping in the urgency of his walk. "I've been looking all over for you kids!"

I saw he was fully dressed again and looked very angry.

"I'm Lieutenant Rawlings," the man introduced himself. "These two belong to you?"

"Yes, they do. I'm Dr. Baylor."

"Oh yes," he said, shaking Dad's hand. "You're the man Captain Jackson spoke with today."

"That's right. I'm sorry my children have caused a problem."

"No real problem, Doctor. The captain and I spotted them from the bridge. Two tykes in pajamas, leaning over the railing. We were a bit worried. But your son tells me they're both good swimmers."

I heard the trace of amusement in his voice, but I saw that actually he was frowning.

"I was just telling them, Dr. Baylor, to be careful, that we won't stop for anyone washed overboard. Wartime regulations and all that, but it's important the kids take it seriously because it's a rule the captain won't break. Not in these waters, at any rate."

"They will trouble you no further," Dad said stiffly.

"Oh look here, Doctor, I didn't mean we expect any trouble from them. We want this trip to be as pleasant as possible for you civilians. The children, especially. I've got kids of my own, so I realize it's going to be impossible to keep them cooped up all the time. But they've got to realize the serious nature of things and stay out of the way. I trust they understand what to do in case of an Alert."

"They do."

The officer looked down at Hugh and me. "You must keep to the areas designated for the civilians. But as long as it's calm and there are so few of you, I think we can relax the deck hours a bit for you kids. But you're not to be up here near the guns."

He turned back to Dad. "Our restrictions mainly pertain to the adults, you see. In case of an emergency, we can't have all sorts of people milling about. But you have grand kids here, Doctor. And one good thing about a ship is, well, you'll always know they're somewhere on it, isn't that right?"

The warmth in his voice seemed calculated to subdue our father's ire, and I was glad to see his expression and stance relax somewhat.

Then to my dismay, the officer added, "I would keep an eye on the girl, however, if I were you. She shouldn't go anywhere alone. We can't testify to the trustworthiness of all of our passengers."

"I'll look after her," Hugh said, which caused both men to smile just a little.

After the officer left us, Hugh looked up at Dad and asked in Donald Duck talk, "You still mad at us?"

But Dad was not amused this time. "Your mother woke up and found you both gone. We were very worried."

"Sorry," we both said.

I was relieved that Dad did not pursue the issue nor hurry us down to the cabin. Instead, he stood with us awhile at the railing and looked out at the dark outline of India that was diminishing in the distance.

For a long while he was silent, but then he said very quietly, "Seven years!"

He sounded sad somehow, and Hugh must have heard it, too, because he grasped my hand tightly to tell me not to say anything right now.

The ship dipped up and down and rolled gently from side to side.

At last Hugh asked, "A good seven years, huh, Dad?"

"I'm not sure. I helped ease the physical suffering of a great many people, yes, but I don't know what I did for their souls."

"*God* knows," I said.

Dad nodded. He held out a hand to each of us. "Let's try to be thoughtful of one another. Your mother's not well. Please don't add to her distress. And she and I will do our best to make you happy, too, in giving you as much freedom as the ship's rules allow.

"But you heard what the man said, Janet," my father went on. "You're not to go anywhere on the ship unless Hugh or one of us is with you."

Yes, sometimes it certainly was a trial being a girl.

# *Three*

The next morning, the boil under my arm was so huge I had to hold my arm out at my side or rest my hand on my hip. Dad took a look at it and said he'd have to lance it after breakfast. I didn't like the sound of that! It worried me so much I could hardly eat. But what did intrigue me at breakfast were the little containers of Kellogg's cereal that could have the milk poured right inside them so you didn't need a bowl. I had one of Corn Flakes and one of Rice Krispies. And a strip of bacon. But I didn't go anywhere near the three different kinds of eggs nor the waffles with syrup, and congratulated myself on my great restraint.

Kevin was with us. He looked haggard. We peppered him with questions about his first night with the Chinese threesome: Did he sleep well? What did they wear to bed? Did he remember to say his prayers? Did he hear the engines come on?

"Mr. Huang snores so loudly, I couldn't hear anything else."

"You were asleep already then," Hugh said, "'cuz it wasn't just the noise, it was the shakes."

"I had a lot of bad dreams," Kevin said.

"What about?" Mother asked.

"I don't remember now."

Hugh told him about our adventure on the deck.

"Next time, if you can get to me," Kevin said, "come and get me. I wouldn't mind going along."

"There will be no more such adventures," Dad said firmly.

Kevin said nothing for a while. He picked a hole in his fried egg and spread the yolk over the white part, but didn't eat it.

"They argue a lot," he said glumly. "I can't understand a word of it, but it sounds like they're arguing. Lee cried. I gather part of the problem was your suggestion that he join us for meals and so forth, Jannie, because later Lee told me his uncle won't let him. But he wouldn't say why."

As I suspected, the lancing of the boil wasn't any fun. First, Dad had me hold a hot washcloth against it for a while to soften it up. Then he took one of his injection needles and poked a hole in it, probing around a bit to make the hole big enough, saying "Steady now!" when I whimpered. Then he pushed the pus out. That part hurt. Mother was there, her comforting hand on my shoulder, and Kevin held one of my ankles, squeezing it once in a while.

When it was over, I felt a lot better. I reluctantly admitted I was getting another boil on my right side, just above my waist.

"I think it's the change in diet," Dad said. "Too many rich foods after Ridge Point's bland fare. Let's keep an eye on that. More vegetables, less fat, that should do the trick."

Eventually it did; in the course of the next five weeks I had four more boils and then never again.

Just as Dad was covering the hole with gauze and a strip of adhesive tape, Hugh came in. He was sorry he'd missed seeing the pus come out. He liked watching things like that.

"There're prisoners on board," he told us.

"Prisoners!" Mother looked alarmed.

"POWs," Hugh said. "Italians. They're up on deck, chipping paint. They've got striped pajamas on."

He went on to tell us he'd talked with one who spoke English, a "really nice guy," whose name was Paolo. The man had told him there were five hundred of them, quartered in the stern on D deck and allowed out only a few at a time.

"He gave me this!" Hugh held up a carving of a giraffe, made from driftwood. It was truly beautiful, the animal's face and the muscles of its slim neck and legs finely depicted.

"He made it for his son," Hugh said.

"Then you must give it back to him!" Mother said sharply.

"Oh no, Mother, he wants me to have it, really. He said he's got plenty of time to make another one. He said he could get a different piece of wood in the work-shop."

"Workshop?" Kevin asked with interest.

"Paolo gets to do stuff there 'cuz he's a carpenter."

"Maybe they'll let me work there, too," Kevin said. He liked making things, and I could see he was pleased at the thought of having something to do.

"I'm not sure I like the idea of you boys being in con-tact with any of these prisoners, though," Mother said, glancing at Dad to see if he would also voice an objec-tion.

Mother's concern in this regard was predictable. Even before the United States entered the war, she and my father had developed a keen suspicion of anyone whose nationality made him or her someone who wasn't "on our side." We had distant relatives in the Netherlands, and there was a lot of talk around our family table about the German occupation of that country, among others, and about the multitudes of Jews and those who had attempted to give them asy-lum who were being herded off to concentration camps. My parents began to say the words "German" and "Nazi" in the same tones of fear and hostility they usually reserved for mention of the Devil, in spite of the fact that until as late as 1942, a German doctor had worked at one of the mission hospitals in the Punjab, and Dad had always spoken of her in respectful terms.

When she left abruptly, there was speculation as to her loyalties. We later heard she had been rounded up with other German civilians in India and had been sent to a detention camp, and that seemed not to bother my parents at all. One never knew where a spy was lurking, they said. No German was to be trusted anymore, and this belief was particularly reinforced when we would listen to recorded portions of Hitler's tirades relayed on the BBC. Now the enemy had a voice, and it was a frightening one, to be sure. Among us, only Dad and Kevin knew a smattering of German, but my not understanding exactly what was being said didn't prevent me from feeling strangely chilly, especially so when the shout of a massive crowd supported Hitler's words with the united cry of "*Sieg heil! Sieg heil!*" When Dad said it meant "Hail to victory" it sounded even more ominous. It was troubling to think of so many faceless enemies, and with the bombing of Pearl Harbor, the crowd of them increased. Now that we were at sea, I imagined one of them putting an eye to a periscope, spotting our ship, and giving the order "to blow us to Kingdom Come," as Hugh had expressed it recently.

In response to Mother's comment, however, Hugh said with a patient sigh, "They're not *criminals,* you know, just Italians. You meet Paolo, you'll see he's a perfectly nice person."

Mother asked pointedly, "Well, Samuel, what do you think?"

He looked at Kevin's eager face. "I think he should

investigate the workshop. *I'm* going to find the printshop and see about this newspaper. I wonder when today's issue will come out? I'd like to see it. I'm thinking of writing an article. What will *you* do this morning, Nellie?"

"I'll stay here and read my book," she said quietly.

She was reading *Gone With the Wind,* and I wished she would hurry up and finish it because I wanted to read it, too. It was awfully big, but I figured I could get through it by the time we got to the States.

"And what will you kids do?" Dad asked Hugh and me.

"I'd like to go find Lee and challenge him to a game of jacks," I said. I was looking forward to that because it was a game I was good at. Almost no one could beat me.

"I'd like him to teach me how to play chess," Hugh said.

I rolled my eyes at the ceiling.

"Okay," he said, "let's go find out what *he'd* like to do."

We found Lee lying on his stomach in his upper bunk, reading. Mr. Huang and Dao-Zeun were hunched over a chessboard.

"Whatcha readin'?" I asked Lee.

He showed us the cover. The embossed title was splotched with mildew.

"*Little Women!* That's a girl's book!" Hugh said.

"It's the only one that looked any good."

61

"Where'd you find it?" I asked.

"In the library."

"Library!"

"There's books in the lounge. They let Uncle and me go in after breakfast. There's books donated by"—he read from the cover page — "the Women's Society of the Evangelical Reformed Church, Elmhurst, Illinois." Lee shrugged. "Never mind about that. I like it. It's about people."

"Can we go there now?" I had hoped to invite him back to our cabin for jacks, and Hugh could join in if he wanted to. But now the thought of investigating a new place that had books in it was much more interesting. Anyway, the floor was a bit tippy for jacks, I realized. They would go scooting, and when you got into the double bouncies you couldn't be reaching under a bunk.

"There's dominos and puzzles, too," Lee told us.

"Well, let's go!" Hugh exclaimed. "Let's see if they'll let us in!"

Lee shot his uncle a worried look, but Mr. Huang was concentrating on a move, and Lee had to wait a while before asking, "May I go, Uncle?"

Mr. Huang muttered something in what I took to be Chinese. When at last he looked up at Lee, his kind brown eyes and his expression registered great concern. Or was it disappointment? His next remark was gently said, but it caused Lee's chin to tighten stubbornly, and he and his uncle engaged in what seemed to me a rapid-fire dialogue. Apparently Lee's uncle was not keen on letting him go. I wondered why not. The man's sweet face did not seem consistent with a refusal to allow his nephew this small freedom.

At length he must have relented, because Lee said to us, "Okay, let's go."

"Tell them what I say, Lee," Mr. Huang said softly. "Good they know rules also."

Lee said, his head hanging a bit, "I must not talk to strangers. If grownups come in, I must go."

"But they won't!" I said. "Not this time of day." I turned to Mr. Huang. "Anyway, we'll be very good. We won't bother anyone."

Mr. Huang nodded, his face impassive now. "Lee knows rules."

And I thought *I* was under strict limits! I wondered if Lee had once upon a time had a sorry experience with an adult. I knew the rule about not talking to strangers, of course. Dad and Mother had often told me there were evil men in the world who liked to do bad things to children. We'd all heard stories of European children who were kidnapped and sold to chieftains in Afghanistan. They liked fair-haired girls the best, people said. My parents took these tales to heart. Wherever I went while I was home on vacation, one of my brothers had to be with me.

But here on board ship, the uncle's rule that Lee had

to leave the room the minute an adult came in seemed particularly harsh and unnecessary. After all, Hugh and I would be with him.

A sailor let us in. The room was dark and stuffy with the smell of mold and furniture polish, beer and stale cigarette smoke. We turned on a couple of lamps with raggedy tasseled shades. One wall was all books with faded covers. On the opposite side of the room was a gleaming bar with a colorful assortment of bottles behind it, and on each wall in between hung a huge oil painting of a ship at sea, one of which was approaching a tropical island, the other clearly in danger of crashing on some rocks. Motley assortments of armchairs had been grouped together in the corners, and in the middle of the room were four solid-looking card tables with raised edges so things wouldn't slide off. A number of sturdy standing ashtrays had been placed here and there.

"Where are the games?" Hugh asked.

Lee pointed to a chest under the painting of the peaceful ship, and the two boys headed for it while I went to look at the bookshelves. After great deliberation, I chose three books that had promising titles: *Safari Terrors, Adventures Amongst the Zulus,* and *Bright Night, Dark Morning.* Then I spotted the magazine rack in another corner. It was full of tattered copies of *The Saturday Evening Post* and *Life,* good for a month of Sundays.

"Come play with us, Janet!" Lee called to me happily. "I'm going to teach you mah-jongg."

He sat at one of the tables and spilled out the box of tiles. They were made of ivory, darkly yellowed with age, and pleasingly smooth and cool to the touch. He showed us the bamboos and circles, the winds and dragons, the flowers and seasons. Later, when he'd taught us the rules and we played our first game, I found I liked the last two prettiest kinds so much I could hardly bear to discard one from my lineup, even if it would mean achieving a *pung* of red dragons.

It was a wonderful game. We'd been playing for two hours or so, and Lee had just shouted another winning "*Woo!*" when he suddenly looked up in alarm at someone who had come into the lounge. He looked so scared, I turned in my chair to see who it was.

It was the European woman. Today, instead of a sari, she was wearing slacks and had coiled her long blond braid on top of her head.

She, too, looked startled, giving Lee a fearful glance before saying directly to Hugh and me, "I'm so sorry! I didn't know you were in here. I came only for a magazine."

Lee said to us, "I must go."

"No, no, *I'll* go," the woman said and left without selecting her magazine.

Hugh and I looked at each other in wonder.

"Do you know her?" Hugh asked Lee.

"How would I know her?" Lee asked sharply.

"I don't know. But you seem to be afraid of each other," Hugh observed.

Lee studiously proceeded to flip over the tiles in preparation for another game. Finally, without glancing up at us, he said, "I've seen her staring at me. At me and Uncle and Dao-Zeun. I think she thinks we're Japanese."

Hugh said impatiently, "That's stupid! We wouldn't let any *Japanese* on this ship!"

Lee bit his lower lip. "Don't tell Uncle, please, or he won't let me play with you again."

Hugh and I agreed we wouldn't tell, but I promised myself to ask that woman, flat out, what her problem was with this small, beautiful boy.

That evening our whole family went to the lounge during the two-hour period allowed to the C-deck passengers.

The second we walked in, Mother murmured, "It's dreadful in here."

With numbers of people there, the room was hot and smelled sweaty. Three groups were playing card games. The atmosphere was hazy with smoke. In a far corner sat the rubber plantation man, who was puffing on an enormous cigar. The yellow-skinned man was not with him.

Mother looked apprehensively at the bar where three men were sitting on stools and laughing together, drinks in hand.

"This is no place for children," she said. "Whatever were we thinking, to imagine we could have our family times here!"

"No one's going to bite us, Mother," Kevin said with a touch of irritation. "Relax."

Dad had already found the magazine rack. He liked the mystery stories in *The Saturday Evening Post,* and I saw he was looking at the dates of a number of issues to be sure he could read all the parts of a serial.

Then I saw the woman. She had changed into a red-and-black patterned caftan and was curled up in a big chair with a book on her lap. But she wasn't reading it. She was staring at the thin line of smoke that rose from the cigarette she held in a long filter.

"I'm going over to talk to that lady," I told Mother.

"Why?" she asked with a frown. She was suspicious of women who smoked.

"She looks lonely."

"I suppose it will be all right," Mother said. "But Janet, I don't think we'll be staying very long."

I took a chair beside the woman and looked down at my bitten nails for a while. (She had lovely long red-polished ones.)

"Hi."

"Hello yourself." She had a nice voice, warm and husky. She had a nice smell, too, not of talcum powder, as Mother did, but of real perfume that reminded me of wild honeysuckle on a rainy day. Her eyes were an intense royal blue, with long black lashes and dark brows that contrasted attractively with her blond hair, which hung loose now, framing her face. It was an aristocratic face, I thought, although my parents had discouraged me from thinking in those terms: Good bones and character in a face, they said, had nothing to do with privilege or poverty.

"I'm Janet Baylor. What's your name?"

"Ann Dobson."

"Pleased to meet you. How come you don't like Lee?"

I had taken her by surprise. Her eyes widened before she looked quickly away and took a puff of her cigarette.

"Is that the boy I saw with you today?" she asked without looking at me.

"The dark-haired one. The other one's my brother."

"Yes, I can see that."

"Lee thinks you're afraid of him because you think he's Japanese."

She gave me an amazed look. "He said *that?*"

"He's not, you know. He's Chinese with other blood mixed in, I think. And I don't think he's making this thing up," I went on. "You gave him *such* a look today!"

"Did I? I didn't mean to. I was simply surprised to find anyone here at that hour."

"That's not how it looked to us," I persisted.

"I'm sorry. Please tell him I think he's a beautiful boy."

"That's what I think, too, but I'm not going to tell him that. Are you married?"

She smiled a bit, showing lovely straight teeth. "Not anymore."

"Did he die?"

"You're very direct, aren't you?"

I nodded. "It's the only way to get answers. I think grownups beat around the bush a lot."

"Perhaps. But I'm sure your mother has told you it's not polite to ask personal questions."

I nodded again. "But I don't know how to ask the other kind. And personal ones are what I'm interested in. You don't have to answer if you don't like."

She was silent awhile. "All right, I'll answer. No, he didn't die. He's very much alive."

"I'll bet he was an Indian."

She burst out laughing.

"He was, wasn't he?" I said, pressing my advantage because I saw she was amused, not condescending, in her mirth. "And that's why you sometimes wear saris," I added, wanting to test my supposition. "I think you look better in Western clothes, though," I told her, quickly adding, "Oh, I thought you looked lovely in the blue-and-gold one last night! But I still think saris look better on Indian women somehow."

"I agree with you," she responded with a warm smile. "But I like wearing them, nevertheless. They're comfortable. Recently, I've worn nothing but saris or the *salvar kurta,*" and I had to agree with her that the latter outfit, especially, the pajamalike pantaloons with the tunic over them, looked comfier than slacks or a dress.

"Did your husband like you to dress like that?"

"Not at all."

"Then why did you?"

"For the past three years I've lived in an *ashram.*"

"Are you a Hindu?" I asked in amazement.

She shook her head.

Why then, I wondered, would she want to live in a Hindu community that probably practiced a certain swami's teachings? (I'd learned about such things in our social studies class.)

"Well then . . . ?" I prompted.

"I just wanted to be there."

It sounded evasive to me. I seemed to be getting into territory she was even less willing to talk about than the subject of her husband, but I was interested in this *ashram* business and asked her if it had been a really strict one.

"Oh no, it was a branch of the Divine Life Society that Swami Sivananda began."

"But why . . ."

"I liked it because it rejects caste. And it emphasizes social service," she added.

"No, I meant . . . well, is that what you came to India for?"

"Not exactly."

I hated answers that didn't go anywhere, but I was reluctant to let this subject drop.

"Where was this *ashram?*" I asked.

"In the Punjab."

This also was a vague answer; the Punjab is a huge territory.

"We lived right near the Punjab," I told her. "In the Northwest Frontier Province."

And now I distinctly saw a wary look in her eyes that had me befuddled because it seemed to me my last comment was merely the sort of thing an adult might have added to keep a polite conversation going.

She tapped a polished thumbnail against a tooth, all the while looking down at her lap. Then she lit another cigarette and blew the first puff at the ceiling in a long, tired breath.

"I've never been that far north," she said. "I was in Lahore and . . . I moved around a good deal."

I imagined the women in *ashrams* had to spend their mornings kneading dough for mountains of *chappattis* or stirring enormous cauldrons of lentils.

"Doing what?" I asked.

"I helped out with the ones who were sick. The women and children."

"Are you a doctor?"

"Oh no," she said quickly, "but I make a very good nurse."

"My mother's a nurse," I informed her. "A really good one. She graduated first in her class. When I got chicken pox, and some of my friends did, too, she came up to the mountains to look after us. But I usually just think of her as Mother. When we're home on vacation, she hardly ever goes to work."

The woman beside me said in a low voice, "I certainly understand that."

I thought she was looking more relaxed now, her blue eyes bright with interest, so I went on: "Anyway, Mother doesn't have to do it if she doesn't want to, 'cause the mission doesn't pay wives, so she can do as she pleases, and I don't think it pleases her all that much. She told me once she'd rather be a teacher. But Dad wanted her to help him stamp out disease, and she was afraid he wouldn't marry her otherwise. He's a doctor, you know."

"Yes, I know. I heard the captain address him yesterday, remember? I was standing near you."

"I saw you. The captain called Dad to his quarters to tell him a secret, but he won't say what it's about. I hate secrets. I always want to know things."

"Yes, you do," she replied with a little smile.

Now was my chance. "Was your husband an Indian or not?"

"Or not. What does the name Dobson sound like to you?"

"Not Indian, I guess, but it could be your maiden name."

"It's my married name."

"So I should call you Mrs. Dobson."

"You may call me Ann, if you like."

"I'd feel better saying Mrs. Dobson. My parents won't let me call adults by their first name. Where were you born?"

Again she looked startled. "Dobson's an *American* name!"

"You don't sound American."

"Perhaps not," she said, looking down at a fingernail. "I don't know what I sound like anymore. I've been speaking almost nothing but Urdu for the last long while."

All right, I thought, here's something I can test her on. She either knows the language or she doesn't; it isn't something she can fudge on. And if she has lived in an Indian community in the Punjab, she probably knows some Punjabi, too.

"The village kids in Taxila taught me a song," I said, and without further preamble, I sailed into it, keeping my voice low so as not to attract attention, although I wouldn't have minded that because I have a nice singing voice and know how to stay on pitch. I thought of it as a silly little song actually, about telling a frog — I imagined him as being old and fat — to go to the edge of a well where he would want to jump into the clear water, tumbling and tumbling until he landed on his head. The fun of it was in the three rhyming words at the ends of the lines, and anyone who knew Urdu or Punjabi would know those.

When I'd finished the song, she touched my hand. "I

like the metaphor," she said quietly, "because a *baba* is a seeker of truth, which the pure water of a well symbolizes. People are like wells, you know. Every one of us is a very deep well."

I thought about that analogy for a while. "And I'm the fat frog that wanted to jump into your well," I responded unhappily.

"You are *not* a fat frog," she said emphatically. "You are an intelligent, attractive girl with an inquiring mind."

That did it. Whatever her mysteries, whatever it was that she seemed so reluctant to talk about, she was my friend.

"Ann Dobson!" Dad said in surprise when I mentioned her name as we were preparing for bed. "Dobson was the name of a doctor who worked in Peshawar, and his wife's name was Ann. He and their infant son were murdered. It occurred a year or so before we arrived in the area."

"How come you never told us about it!" Hugh exclaimed.

"It was not an incident your mother and I wanted to dwell on."

"What happened to his wife?" I asked with interest.

"She disappeared. People thought she'd been kidnapped, but no one knew for certain what became of her."

"You've gotta tell us, Dad," Hugh said, "why the doctor and the baby were murdered."

"According to the report I heard," Dad replied, "Dr. Dobson operated on a Pathan woman whose husband had brought her in to the hospital. She was in great pain and was bleeding profusely. The removal of her uterus stopped the bleeding, but he found the cancer itself was already widespread."

"Oh, I know!" Hugh put in. " 'The operation was a success, but the patient died.' " It was something he'd heard Dad say as an example of the black humor doctors sometimes indulge in, and obviously it had tickled Hugh's fancy because this wasn't the first time he'd repeated it.

"Yes, she died a few weeks later," Dad went on. "And the night after the woman's death, someone pounded on the door of the Dobsons' bungalow, and the doctor, holding his infant son in his arms, went to see who it was. The Pathan man, apparently believing Dobson to be the cause of his wife's death, had come to seek revenge. He decapitated both the doctor and the baby."

"Cut off their heads!" I exclaimed in horror. "Right there on the doorstep?"

"That's right," Dad said soberly. "With his *kukri*. You know we've heard a good deal about the Pathans still insisting on exacting 'an eye for an eye, a tooth for a tooth,' and evidently it's an internal tribal system of justice the British have been able to exert little control over."

"But the doctor's wife . . . ?" I asked in suspense.

"Servants found the bodies . . ."

"And the heads?" Hugh inserted.

". . . the bodies and the heads early the next morning. But the doctor's wife was gone. Vanished."

"Well, then, that's her!" I said excitedly. "She's turned up again!"

"I don't think so," Dad said. "I saw a picture of the missing Ann Dobson. She was dark-haired."

"She could have dyed it blond," Mother suggested.

Dad shook his head. "The Ann Dobson you were talking with tonight, Janet, is not the same woman whose photo I saw. Her age looks about right, that's true, in her late thirties now, and the bones of her face are remarkably similar, but there's one significant difference. Dr. Dobson's wife had a glass eye."

"How could you tell, just from a photograph?" Hugh wanted to know.

"You can tell. There's life in the real eye. And when I mentioned it to one of Dobson's colleagues, he confirmed it. As an infant, she'd developed a tumor close to the right optic nerve, and in removing it, the eye also had to come out."

"My lady doesn't have a glass eye, that's for sure," I said. "She has pretty blue eyes with lots of life in both of them."

Mother gave an impatient little grunt. She seemed

suddenly sick of the subject and said with a shrug, "Ann Dobson isn't such an unusual name, is it? Quite simply, there must be two of them. Anyway, I think we've had enough talk about all of this. It's time for bed."

"Oh, Mother, I can't sleep right now!" I protested. "And it's our time to be on deck! Please let's go up a while! Please, Daddy?"

"We're already in our pajamas," Dad said.

"That doesn't matter. It'll be dark."

"All right. I'll slip my trousers back on. What do you say, Nellie? Shall we get a breath of fresh air?"

Being on deck was always a special experience. I liked the damp breeze licking my face and lifting my hair. I liked the heaving deck, cool under my bare feet, and the great swells of the ocean, looming and subsiding, endlessly, as far as the eye could see. But tonight it was very dark, with no friendly lights on deck, of course, nor any visible in the cloud-covered sky. I guessed the captain must have developed the night vision of an owl by now to be able to steer this ship in such utter darkness.

Very few people had taken advantage of this allotted hour for the C-deck passengers. Kevin hadn't come up either, although he knew the schedule and could have been with us if he wanted.

"I'm going down to get him," Hugh said. "Okay, Dad? You wanna come with me, Jannie?"

Hugh and I were climbing down the final ladder when the alarm went off. BEH–BEH–BEH–BEH!

"Let's go back to our cabin," Hugh said. "Dad and Mother will come down."

They did, just two or three minutes after we got there, and were relieved to see us.

I suggest we all get fully dressed again," Dad said. "You never know . . ."

We pulled our survival kits out from under the bunks. There was no point in checking their contents again. We put the bags in a little heap on the floor between the bunks.

"I wish we'd gotten to Kevin in time," Hugh said. "He'd be with us now. I wonder what he's thinking?"

Hugh and I sat on my lower bunk and held hands. Dad and Mother sat on her bunk together. Dad patted her knee.

The alarm was abruptly turned off. We grinned at each other, waiting to hear the All Clear hoot.

Silence. We were silent, too. The ship creaked and groaned all around us.

I strained my ears to catch a hint of what might be happening in the world overhead. Nothing, except for an occasional thump. It was spooky. The various alarms had promised to be scary when they sounded, but at least they would be signals to tell us the degree of danger. This silence told us nothing. Did it mean hope or fear? Relief or a coming disaster? Why weren't they telling us either to relax or prepare to abandon ship?

" 'The Lord is my shepherd . . .' " Mother began.

We all knew the Twenty-third Psalm by heart, and now we solemnly recited it together.

I felt particularly solemn by the time we got to the verse that said " '. . . Yea, though I walk through the valley of the shadow of death, I shall fear no evil, for Thou art with me. Thy rod and Thy staff, they comfort me . . .' " It wasn't true that I feared "no evil"; I was feeling pretty scared. I tried to compare myself to a sheep that took comfort in the presence of the shepherd, who used his rod to chase away wolves and his crooked staff to grab a wayward sheep by the neck when it wandered too close to a cliff, but here in the cabin I felt cooped up, airless, and far out of the sight of the heavens. " '. . . in the presence of my enemies . . .' " Yes, but where were they? And what would they do to us? A wolf would leap to tear my throat out, but at least I could try to fight back. A sheep wouldn't, of course, but *I* would! Then I liked the part that said " '. . . goodness and mercy shall follow me all the days of my life . . .' " That made it sound as though I still had a few days to live. " '. . . and I shall dwell in the house of the Lord forever,' " the psalm concluded. I didn't mind the idea of living "in the house of the Lord" someday, whatever that meant, but I didn't really want to go there right this minute. I had things I wanted to do first, down here on earth. Did God know that?

"Janet, do you want to say the family prayer tonight?" Dad asked quietly.

"No," I said, "that psalm was good enough."

No one disputed that, and we sat in silence a long time.

I thought it would be nice if the captain would talk to us, as the chef had. Trapped here below the decks of freedom, it would be good to be in touch with the knowledge of the captain on his all-seeing, all-knowing bridge. *He* was our god now. It was he who would ultimately determine if we needed to stay put or run to our lifeboats. Why didn't he say something or give us a clue?

God was like that, too, I thought. You could pray and pray about something and wait months sometimes before you got an answer, which often was "No!" Mother said the secret was in knowing what to ask for. You didn't pray for good health, for instance, but for the wisdom to conduct your life healthfully. But even that was no guarantee, it seemed to me, because germs or what-have-you could grab you at any time, no matter how careful you were, so then when you were sick, Mother said, you prayed for the patience to endure it, and if it got worse than that, you prayed for peace of mind about going to meet the Lord, which was where we were all headed for, so it didn't matter if it happened early or late in life, which was fine for her to say because she'd already lived thirty-nine whole years, but I wasn't even ten yet.

About an hour later we heard the All Clear.

# Four

The next morning at breakfast we were told our ship had spotted an aircraft carrier on the horizon, and the carrier had spotted us, as well, sending its planes dipping over us to determine our identity. It had taken some time for the two ships to recognize each other as Allies.

"I'll bet all the Allies have secret codes," Hugh said.

"Then why did it take so long?" I asked.

"No one can trust anyone these days," Hugh said. "Codes can be decoded. But people want to be cautious before they start letting bombs or artillery fly."

"I like the idea of bombs better than torpedoes, don't you?"

He thought about that. "I guess so. A bomb would get the sailors up top, but a torpedo would blow a hole closer to us, and the ship might go down before we had a chance to get out."

Mother laid her fork down on top of a half-eaten

pancake. "I wish you children would *stop* these dreadful speculations!"

Dad covered her hand with his and said gently, "They're chasing goblins, Nellie. It's a necessary exercise."

Petty Officer Mike Turner came to our cabin that evening, wearing tropical whites, the V-shaped stripes now in deep blue, stitched to his short sleeves. He told us we were about to cross the Equator, and for a second I thought of it as a line I might be able to see.

He was carrying a brown paper bag and told Hugh and me to make laps onto which he dumped numerous packets of Wrigley's gum and Hershey bars with almonds in them.

"My goodness, Mike, you mustn't!" Mother exclaimed.

"No problem, Ma'am," Mike said with a happy grin, "I get this stuff cheap at the PX. Say, there's perfume there, too. I got my mom some. Chanel Number Five, it's called. Think she'll like it?"

"Oh my, I'm sure she will!" Mother said.

Mike said he had the evening off and would be glad to take Hugh and me to the deck aft where the day's garbage was dumped from, which was probably going on right now, if we kids were interested.

We were. We found the swabbies working at emptying out the great containers by starlight, as it wasn't cloudy that night. Who would have believed such vast amounts of garbage could be just one day's accumulation! Swosh! there went another upended barrelful, and the fish leaped in the froth.

"Hey! There were utensils in that one!" Hugh exclaimed. "I saw knives and forks!"

"Yeah," Mike said languidly, "they don't always watch for that when they scrape the dishes off."

We watched the fish again for a while. Out beyond them, the white wake of the ship looked like the trail of a giant sea snake, and Mike explained that the captain was under orders to pursue a zigzagging course as often as possible to make us less of an easy target for torpedoes.

"Mike, can I ask you a question?" Hugh said.

"Shoot."

"There aren't enough lifeboats for everyone, are there?"

Mike took off his cap and scratched his head. "Sure there are. What makes you think there aren't?"

"We were told twenty people per boat. They said enough drinking water for twenty for fourteen days and . . ."

"Oh, I get yer drift! But the point is, they don't expect anything like that to last fourteen days, so there could be forty in a boat, you see? You get my meaning?"

"That would be pretty squeezy," I remarked.

"Yup."

"Do you think after the Japs got us, they'd stop and pick us up?" I asked.

"What mouse brought that kernel out?"

I told him about our cousin Jimmy's friend being rescued by Germans.

Mike said thoughtfully, "I've heard of things like that, sure, but I don't think you can reckon on it. But look here, you kids ought not to be scarin' yerselves like that. That's just flappin' yer wings in the breeze, goin' nowhere."

He put a hand on Hugh's shoulder and held out the other to me.

"Let's be gettin' you back home. Stinks here. Sky's pretty though, hunh? Pretty soon the moon'll be up, the first little scrap of it. Maybe next time it comes 'round, we'll be kissin' our grannies."

When we got to our cabin door, Mike said, "Y'all rest easy tonight, you hear? And tell your mom I think she's just about the nicest person I've had the pleasure of meetin'."

Three nights later, the Alert sounded again. Without being in Mike's company, Hugh and I had gone to watch the "garbage detail," as the swabbies called it. When the BEH–BEH–BEH–BEH came over the loudspeaker on the rear deck, one of the young men yelled at us, "Run! Get back where you belong!"

We raced to C deck, but we were far from our cabin, and Hugh thought we should take temporary refuge, as the captain had told us to do in this sort of situation.

We knocked on a cabin door, and a man shouted, "Come in!"

The man was bending over another man who was sitting in a wobbly fashion on a lower bunk. The bending man looked up, his face taut with worry.

It was my rubber plantation man and his bad-liver friend, whose face was now the color of bathtub scum, his brown-and-yellow eyes wide with a kind of confused terror. His strong, deeply tanned friend was supporting him with one arm and was trying to pull a lifebelt over his head with the other.

"Help me with this thing!"

Hugh stepped up and adjusted the lifebelt across the man's chest.

The alarm continued to sound insistently.

Hugh said, "He should lie down again. We should elevate his feet."

When the two of them had the man comfortably down again with a blanket over him and pillows under his feet, Hugh sat on the bunk next to him and laid his fingertips on the man's nearest wrist, taking his pulse. (Hugh liked doing the little doctor things Dad had taught him how to do.) "His heart's skipping beats like crazy, but his color's getting a whole lot better," he pronounced.

It was true — the man's face was not quite so gray as it had been; it had taken on the shade of a tired grapefruit.

The tanned man sat on the opposite lower bunk, buried his face in his hands, and shuddered.

I sat down next to him. "He should be in the infirmary where the ship's doctor can look after him."

"He won't have anything to do with doctors. He's made me promise not to take him to the ship's doctor against his will."

"But he's awfully sick, Mr. . . . . I don't know your name."

"Patrick McCullough."

"I'm Janet Baylor. And that's my brother Hugh."

"The doc's kids, hunh? I might have guessed."

"Why's your yellow friend so allergic to doctors?"

Mr. McCullough frowned at me. "His name is Bob Caldwell."

"Oh. Okay."

"For the past seven years he's been teaching at the School for the Blind in Dehra Dun."

"That's nice."

"He doesn't talk much." He sighed and added, "But he vomits a lot."

Hugh said sympathetically, "He's lucky to have a good friend looking after him."

"We only just met when we came on board," Mr. McCullough replied in a gruff tone.

"Oh," said Hugh. "Then I'm surprised you put up with it."

Mr. McCullough gave him a sharp look. "I don't have much choice. I promised, so I'm stuck with it."

Changing my wording a bit, I asked again, "But *why* doesn't he like doctors?" (I couldn't imagine anyone not liking my dad, for instance, and I assumed all doctors were like him.)

"He's had a couple of bad experiences with them, I guess," Mr. McCullough replied. "Or maybe it's got something to do with his religion. I don't know, really. He didn't go into details."

The alarm was silenced. Mr. Caldwell was sleeping now. We three sat quietly for a few minutes, waiting for the All Clear to sound, but it didn't.

"Mr. McCullough," I said, "can I ask you something else?"

"I suppose so."

"Were you ever the manager of a rubber plantation in Burma?"

He gave a sharp burst of laughter.

"Guess not," I said.

"What in heaven's name gave you that notion?"

"You look like an outdoors person. I thought maybe . . . So what *do* you do? I hope you don't mind me asking, but I've wanted to know ever since I first saw you."

"Why?"

"Well," I said, feeling a bit silly, "I made up a story about you. But I bet *your* story's even better," I added encouragingly.

He turned his head away. After a time he answered in a dull voice, "I'm a herpetologist."

Hugh looked up in interest.

"I don't know that word," I said.

"Snakes," Hugh said. "He studies snakes and other reptiles."

This *is* better! I thought.

Mr. McCullough was regarding Hugh with a new look of appreciation in his eyes. "You know that word, do you?"

"Sure, it's what I want to be someday."

"You said you wanted to be a biology teacher," I reminded him.

"There's no reason I can't do both, Jannie."

I turned to Mr. McCullough. "Hugh's nuts about snakes. He captured a cobra once, and his biology teacher cooked it and made sandwiches for the whole class. And once I almost stepped on a krait," I continued in a rush, wanting the man to know I'd had my own encounters with poisonous snakes, and suddenly I clearly recalled the little dust-colored viper on the path of our garden at home in Taxila and the vigor with which the *mali*, our gardener, had killed it, exclaiming as he did so that this type was responsible for hundreds of deaths each year in India.

"And once when my dad was tucking me in," I went on, "he saw a cobra in my bed and yanked me out just in time."

Mr. McCullough was frowning.

"You don't believe me," I said, feeling miffed.

"I believe you," he responded quietly.

Encouraged by this, I went on to tell him about one afternoon in Taxila, when I was five and not yet sent away to school, I was standing near the *mali* on the verandah as he lowered the bamboo blinds, and a cobra fell right at my feet.

"I think it must've been taking a nap inside the rolled-up chics," I said, "'cuz it was stunned a bit when it fell, and 'fore it raised its head, the *mali* chopped it off."

Mr. McCullough made no comment.

"He chopped it off with the machete he always carried," I said, hoping to stir his interest. "I guess that's why you used to have that *kukri* with you, huh?"

Still he said nothing.

"It was scary! I could've been bitten!"

He glanced at me, and I saw his eyes were glistening with tears. "My wife was bitten by a cobra," he said softly.

Oh gosh, I thought, a lump instantly rising in my throat, that means she died! Dad once said there was nothing to be done about a cobra bite, that usually the person was dead already by the time people could get him to the hospital. She died! So that explains . . . I glanced desperately across the cabin at Hugh.

"I'm so sorry," he murmured for both of us.

Mr. McCullough was silent for quite some time before he said, "It's over now." He touched my hand with one finger. "It's not a good story, kids. We were a team,

89

Alison and I, sent out by . . . You know Chicago? You ever been there?"

Hugh shook his head. "We've never been anywhere."

"Well, go sometime and see the Field Museum. That's who sent us out. To collect snakes. Alison was fearless. I warned her. She was very good, you know, very good at her work. But she was fearless," he repeated with a slow shake of his head. He lapsed into silence again.

I imagined her — What had she looked like, this woman who hadn't minded snakes? — I imagined her walking fearlessly through tall grass and suddenly the hooded head of a king cobra rising above it, the eyes red in the little pinched face like a bat's, and then the lightning-swift strike. Oh!

"How come she wasn't afraid?" I asked tentatively. "A cobra can pop up anywhere."

"It wasn't like that," he said soberly. "This one was in a cage."

"Then — How come . . . ?"

"Bloody careless, in the end, that's how," he said bitterly. "She thought she knew it well enough."

He stared at the floor and ventured nothing more.

I looked at Hugh, whose intelligent blue eyes were riveted on Mr. McCullough.

After a time, perhaps because he also realized the man was one of those adults who needed help to keep a conversation going, Hugh asked, "You kept cobras in cages, huh?"

Mr. McCullough looked up sharply, as though Hugh and I had just appeared in his cabin. "Uh, very few. Not only cobras."

"To study, you said. Tell me about that," Hugh said. "I mean, snakes in cages don't do much, do they? So what do you look at?"

Mr. McCullough gave Hugh a little smile. "You're right, usually we studied them in their own habitats. In order to display anything, reptiles or animals or birds, the museum needs lots of information besides the specimen itself. So whenever we found one — any one of the snakes on our list and some that were new to us — we tracked it and studied its total environment. Took photos. Drew pictures. And of course there were a certain number we had to take back with us."

"Alive!" I exclaimed.

"Oh no," he said quickly, "just the skeletons and skins. There are people who reconstruct them back home. And there are others who look at the photos to make the display real. I don't have anything to do with that part. But they're very good at it."

I asked, "You got snake bones and skins in here? Can we see 'em?"

He shook his head. "All in storage. Two hundred and fifty-seven specimens and more than two thousand photographs."

"Wow!" Hugh's eyes were full of admiration for the man. "I wish I could go with you next time. When you go back for more."

"I'm never going back to India," he said curtly. "I never want to see the place again."

I guessed going back to India would give him sad thoughts about his wife. I chewed a fingernail awhile and then said cautiously, "You haven't said how she . . . how it happened."

"A bite on the hand. When she reached into the cage. That simple," he said, showing no emotion now.

"Oh." I tried to picture it. I thought that if she'd been so good at her work, that had been a pretty stupid thing to do. But then, he'd practically said the same thing himself; she'd gotten careless. Too confident, maybe. Too fearless. It's good to be a bit fearful sometimes, I thought; it helps to keep your wits about you.

Hugh spoke up, "My dad says bites on the hand are worse than the feet."

"He's right," Mr. McCullough grumbled. "Head and neck worst of all. But then, you realize, with some snakes it doesn't matter where the bite is."

I thought about this awhile and finally asked, "What made you want to have anything to do with them in the first place?"

"The challenge of it," he replied simply. Then he sighed. "Ego, too, partly, I think."

I was pleased I knew that word. I knew at least it had

something to do with needing to prove yourself. Dad said it was a good thing to have as long as you didn't overdo it. It wasn't good, he said, if you pushed it at someone else's expense. He also said it was a private thing people didn't like talking about, so I didn't dare ask Mr. McCullough what his ego had to do with snakes. As far as I was concerned, a person would have to be pretty brave to be around poisonous snakes for a living, so maybe it was bravery he needed to prove to himself.

The All Clear sounded, and Mr. Caldwell groaned and stirred on his bunk. Hugh, who was still sitting beside him, laid a hand gently on his forehead. "He's got a terrific fever."

"Time I gave him another cool sponge bath," Mr. McCullough said. "You kids better go. Your parents will be worried about you."

"They sure will be," I said earnestly.

As we got up to go, Mr. McCullough said, "You're great kids. I've enjoyed your company."

"It was nice meeting you," Hugh said. (He was very good at remembering the manners Mother had taught us.)

We returned to our cabin where we found our parents stern-faced in their concern about us.

We told them excitedly about our visit with Mr. McCullough and his sick friend.

Mother said, "I don't want you out again after dark."

Dad said, "I'm not keen on your being near Mr. Caldwell. He has hepatitis."

"Is it catching?" I asked.

"Well, not just by being in the cabin with him," Dad admitted. "The disease isn't air-borne. If you drank from the same glass, you might contract his disease. Or if you cleaned up his vomit and forgot to wash your hands afterward."

"I hope Mr. McCullough knows that," Hugh said, "because he told us he cleans up after him all the time."

I said, "You better wash your hands, Hugh, 'cause you touched him. Maybe there were germs on him."

"Touched him?" Dad asked sharply. "Where?"

"Just his wrist and his forehead, Dad."

"Well, even so, Janet's right, please do wash your hands thoroughly, right this minute."

As Hugh went to the sink, Dad said softly, "I doubt Mr. Caldwell will survive this trip."

The following morning we were told the alarm had sounded because of smoke in the Italian prisoners' quarters. One of them had gotten into his bunk with a lighted cigarette and had fallen asleep, setting his bedding on fire.

"There's just *nothing* good to be said for that habit!" Mother said in exasperation.

During the course of the next few days, there were

six more fires. We were not always informed of the cause of them, but each time one occurred, the Alert sent us to our cabin, where we waited in fear as we prayed, not knowing why we were there, and wondering, as the occasions repeated themselves, if one of these times our sojourn through "the valley of the shadow of death" would come to an abrupt end.

# Five

One day Mike came to our cabin and informed us that Mr. McCullough had struck a match on deck the previous night and, as the captain had warned, was put in the brig.

"Good," Mother said. "I hope he stays there. Without his cigar, the lounge will be a good deal more tolerable."

Hugh was frowning. "I'm sorry, because I like him a lot."

"Me, too," I put in.

"Just because he smokes a cigar . . . Well, Mother, if you got to know him, you'd see he's really a very nice man. And now who's going to look after Mr. Caldwell?"

"He's in the sick bay," Mike told us.

"But Mr. McCullough said his friend refused to go there!"

"I hear Caldwell's lower than a lizard's belly,"

Mike said, "and not likely to be puttin' up much of a fuss."

Two days later we heard that Mr. Caldwell had died.

Hugh said at dinner, "Mike says they slipped him overboard last night, out from under a flag. Shark food, huh, Kevin?"

"I don't like that kind of talk," Mother said. "Whoever he was, he was a human soul who is now with the Lord."

I asked, "On Resurrection Day, do you suppose all those bones from the bottom of the ocean will rise to the top?"

"'Dem bones, dem bones, dem *dry* bones!'" Kevin and Hugh started to sing together.

"These won't be dry," I said.

Mother shook her head in disapproval. "You children have the most *lugubrious* imagination lately!"

"Oh, I like that word!" Hugh said. "What does it mean?"

"Macabre," Kevin said.

"And what's *that?*" I inquired.

"Strange and dark and morbid," Dad told me. Unlike Mother, he didn't look upset. "Your mother thinks you dwell on the subject of death too much. I suggest we all go to the lounge tonight and play Monopoly and think about something banal like money."

Mrs. Dobson was there, sitting on a stool at the bar, alone. In front of her was a Y-shaped glass with a little onion lying at the bottom of the clear liquid. Never before had I seen an onion in a drink! I was curious to know what it was and to taste it.

Since Monopoly's best with only four playing, I said I would like to talk with her awhile.

"Not at the bar, you won't," Mother said.

"It's okay, Mother, I'll have Coca-Cola."

"It's not that, it's the principle of the thing."

"All right, I'll ask her if she'll sit somewhere else."

I stood beside Mrs. Dobson. "Hi. I haven't seen you in a while. I've come to say hello. But I'm not allowed to sit on one of these stools."

She looked amused. Without a word, she picked up her glass and preceded me to a cluster of chairs in a corner that was farthest away from my family. Under her lifebelt she wore a white silk blouse tucked into dark blue slacks, and looked very trim from behind, I thought.

"Oh, we didn't order your Coke," she said as she set her drink down, and I realized she had heard us.

"It's okay, I'll have a sip of yours, if I may."

"Your mother will *not* approve," she said very quietly.

"Just a *sip!*" I said even more quietly.

It tasted like pine needle juice. It was dreadful! I told her so.

She nodded. "It takes getting used to."

"That's what my dad says about olives. He didn't get to like them until he was nearly thirty. What I'd like to know is why anyone would keep trying something they hated in the first place."

"Adults do strange things sometimes," she commented.

"You can say that again!"

"No, once is enough."

It was an old joke, but I laughed a bit anyway.

"My dad used to know someone with your exact same name," I told her abruptly. "Well, he didn't exactly *know* her, but he heard about her and he saw a picture of her and he says the two of you look a lot alike, even. Amazing, huh?"

She was looking straight at me, and I expected a big reaction to this piece of news, but nothing much showed on her face except for a little narrowing of her eyes and a flicker of her jaw muscles under the ears.

"Well, don't you want to hear about it?" I asked in some exasperation.

She nodded.

I said eagerly, "The other Ann Dobson was kidnapped by Pathans! I thought it might be you, but Dad said no, the other one had a glass eye."

Now I saw a gratifying flash of interest. I went on, "He notices stuff like that 'cuz he's a doctor. That other Ann Dobson's husband was a doctor, too. What did your husband do?"

It took her a while to answer. She stroked her cheek

with one long polished fingernail, as though she were trying to remember. At length she said in a dull voice, "He was in the import-export business."

"Oh." She was right; it sounded dull to me, too. "Persian rugs and things?" I asked to keep the conversation going.

"Things like that, yes."

Now it was my turn to be quiet while I considered this response. I'd learned not to trust people who gave answers that didn't tell you anything.

"You're not telling me the truth," I said flatly, turning away in my chair.

"But I am!" She touched my knee as though imploring me to believe her. "Persian rugs and things, yes, but mostly he dealt in gems. Look here, I have two with me."

She glanced across the room at my family. Kevin and Hugh were arguing about hotels and railroads, and Mother and Dad were counting out stacks of fake money.

Mrs. Dobson took a tiny embroidered purse from the pocket of her slacks.

"I always carry these with me," she said as she removed a folded square of tissue paper. Inside was cottonwool, and between its layers lay two gems as big as beans, green and blue, an emerald and a sapphire, worth a lot of money, I guessed.

"The last two," she said with a sigh.

I asked the next logical question.

She seemed to be debating with herself again before she replied, "Four. I sold two. They were all I had to live on. They were all my husband left me."

"But I thought . . ." I began. "I heard people can live in *ashrams* for practically nothing, long as they work."

"I had other expenses. But please don't ask me about that, Janet," she added hastily. "I can't tell you that part, at least not quite yet. Perhaps someday I will."

She must have seen the curiosity and disappointment in my face, because she laid her hand firmly on my knee this time and said, "You told me you don't like secrets, but can you *keep* one if I tell you?"

"Yes!"

"All right. My husband didn't give me the gems; I took them from him. I stole them, you might say. I can see you're shocked about that, but he was a . . . not a very nice man, Janet, and when I suspected he was going to leave me without support for . . . when I saw he was going to renege on his responsibilities, I took four of his best gems. And then I swallowed them," she went on with a smile, as though pleased with herself. "He beat me, but he didn't find them!"

"Mr. Dobson *beat* you!"

"Mr. . . . ? uh . . . yes, he did. He certainly did."

"Gosh."

I couldn't imagine my father laying an angry hand on my mother, but once in a while I'd heard angry voices from the Indian quarters not far from our house and then, Smack! and Smack! again, and a woman's cry, sometimes a scream, and Mother would say, "That devil!" so I knew there were men like that, men who could do such things, and if . . .

"You pooped 'em out later, huh?" I asked with a giggle.

Mrs. Dobson squeezed my knee in reply.

"But why did you ever marry such a person in the first place?" I wanted to know.

"I wasn't much of an adult at the time, I can tell you," she replied in a dull voice.

Now she put her hands on mine and said earnestly, "I like you very much, Janet. I like talking with you. Very much. And I trust you. This is our secret, remember? And that means you don't tell your father and mother about it. Is that a promise?"

I nodded solemnly, but I was glad she hadn't mentioned my brothers just now because I had every intention of telling them the second I got a chance to talk to them privately.

"It would be dangerous for me," she continued. "Dangerous in so many ways," she repeated, staring up at the painting of the ship near the rocks. "If your parents were to tell . . ."

I immediately protested, "My parents would never do anything to get you in danger!"

"Oh, you are such a dear little lamb," she said, shaking her head sadly. "So innocent!"

"She *looks* nice," Kevin said when I'd told him and Hugh the following day about my conversation with Mrs. Dobson, "but there certainly seems to be something fishy going on!"

"Yeah," Hugh put in, "I don't believe for a minute there's two people named Ann Dobson. Maybe in the *world,* but not both of them in India! Maybe Dad was wrong about that glass eye."

"But he said Dr. Dobson's colleague confirmed it," Kevin reminded us.

Hugh shook his head dubiously. "I'll bet she's the one that got kidnapped. Sounds to me like she's been hidin' out in these *ashrams.*"

"Sounds to me like she's afraid of her husband," Kevin remarked. "Okay, look, maybe she *is* the same Ann Dobson from Peshawar. She got kidnapped but managed to escape. And then later she married this import-export guy that she took the gems from, and he's been after her ever since. And that's why she said to you, Jannie, that it would be dangerous if you told anyone about it, because she doesn't want him to find her."

I said eagerly, "That's why she looked at me so funny when I said 'Mr. Dobson,' 'cuz she's using her old married name from long ago!"

Kevin sighed. "I still wonder about that glass eye, though. Dad's never wrong about stuff like that."

"We'll know by the time we get to California," I said firmly.

103

I was eager to play a game with Lee again, but Hugh said no, he would rather go up on the deck where the Italians were chipping paint and talk to Paolo if he was there, and Kevin announced his intention to go to the workshop. He was making something, he wouldn't say what, but he'd spent a number of hours on it already and was hoping to complete the project within the next few days. I begged him to tell us what it was, but he said it was a secret.

Another secret! I thought grumpily.

I returned to our cabin, which seemed stuffier than ever. Mother was there, deeply involved in the last pages of her book. Dad was gone. She said he'd found a place on the aft deck where he was working on a piece of writing for the newspaper's Personal Page.

"Funny place to work, near the garbage cans," I said.

"He says it's quite pleasant. Shady, with a nice little breeze back there."

Well then, what was *I* to do? I could read, too, of course, but I wasn't really enjoying my books from the library. Or I could work on my knitting. Mother had taught me to knit when I was five, and I was halfway through making a scarf for my father's birthday. But that wasn't coming up until next November, and it was hard to imagine he would ever feel cold enough to want to wear it, in spite of Mother's assurances that he would be grateful for it when it snowed in Michigan. I had never seen snow, not falling, at any rate. Although I'd often seen vestiges of it at the base of rocks in the Himalayas when we would return for a new school year in February, I had no idea what a snowy day in Michigan might be like.

"I want to play with Lee," I said.

"I don't want you going there by yourself," Mother said, "and I don't like the idea of your being there without Hugh or Kevin present."

"Then *you* come with me!"

Mother ignored me. She wanted to get on with her book, I could see that.

"Mother!"

"What?" she answered absently as she went on reading.

"I *want* to go see Lee!"

Not looking up from her page, she said, "You sound like a four-year-old, Janet."

"I'm bored!"

Now she put her book down. "I always find it such a pity to hear an intelligent person say she's bored. It indicates a singular lack of imagination."

She had said it mildly, not in a stern tone of rebuke, but it stung.

"I *do too* have an imagination!" I objected.

"Then why don't you use it."

"Not just *now!* I want to *play!*"

Mother closed her book and reached for her shoes. I'd won.

"I'll walk over to Lee's cabin with you, Janet," she said in her Let's-be-patient-with-each-other voice, "and we'll see if he can come here to play."

Perhaps Lee had not been acting his age either, because Mr. Huang seemed delighted to let him accompany us back to our cabin, apparently having no objections to Lee's being in the company of adults like my parents. I still wondered about his uncle's stipulation of the other day, however, and I intended to ask Lee about it. I sensed he might tell me if no one else were around. But today Mother would be in the cabin with us, and it would be no good for Lee and me to try to whisper together, since there's nothing that makes a mother perk up her ears so readily as whispering does.

I showed Lee my knitting, and he immediately seized on a skein of the wool that was to go into my father's scarf and used it instead to teach me how to make a macramé hanging for a pot.

"An elf's pot," he said with a mysterious little smile, "not a big witch's one."

I'd been told elves and witches were born in Europe, so I wondered how he'd heard of them, and he said in answer to my question, "I had a teacher once who believed in them."

"A teacher who *believed* . . . ?" I asked in amazement. My own teachers had always made a clear distinction between the factual and make-believe worlds, and I met with this same dichotomy at home: Santa Claus, for instance, was a sweet idea, but it was really your parents who gave you presents, and, anyway, Christmas was about the birthday of Jesus, not about the coming of Santa. Easter, as well, had nothing to do with such frivolous things as bunnies and eggs.

I asked Lee the name of this amazing teacher, but he couldn't remember. He said he'd had a lot of teachers at his boarding school in Darjeeling.

"I went to boarding school, too! Was yours in the mountains, like mine?"

"Sort of."

"Mountains aren't 'sort of,' " I scoffed.

"There were lots of tea bushes around."

"*Everyone* knows *that* about Darjeeling, Lee!" I said impatiently. "But where was your *school?* In the middle of the *tea* bushes?" I went into a giggling fit.

Mother, who was reading her book, looked up and said, "Don't badger him, Janet."

"But Mother . . . !"

"Let him tell you things in his own good time."

"But he's *so bloody* . . . !"

I was searching for the so-bloody *what,* when Mother interrupted to say that wasn't a nice word.

Just then, Dad came in, looking pink-cheeked and happy. I think he noticed there had been words of contention between Mother and me, because he said, "Come with me to look at the sunset, Nellie. There's a refreshing breeze."

The second they'd left, I said to Lee, "I want to know all about you! Where are your parents? And why can't

107

you be in the lounge when people come in? And how come you can't remember that teacher's name!"

Lee didn't answer. He began to untie the macramé holder for the elf's pot, and I watched in fascination, believing he intended to show me something different that could be done with the wool.

At length, without looking up at me, he said in a bitter tone, "Your teeth are like a badger's, too."

I think I must have turned pale. Maybe I blushed. I don't know. But I felt awful. I tend to get quiet when my feelings are hurt, just as I do when I'm scared, so I sat absolutely silent for a while, watching his dexterous fingers work with the wool.

Finally I said, "Not fair to pick on something I can't help."

Now he looked up with a flash of anger. "But you *can* help not sticking your *big nose* in other people's business!"

Oh. This was something else. This meant two things, I knew that, and I didn't like the meaning of either of them.

"Just wanted to know . . ." I began meekly.

He threw the wool down on the floor. "You *can't* know!" he said in a rage, grabbing his hair and pulling it up to the top of his head.

There were holes in his earlobes!

"Hey!" I exclaimed. "You've got . . . you're not . . ."

Lee jumped up and raced to the door.

I leaped up, too, and as Lee ran down the corridor, I screamed after him, "You're not a boy! You're a *girl!*"

"What difference does it make, Jannie?" Hugh said when I told my family about it that evening over supper.

"Because he . . . 'cause he wasn't . . ."

I was embarrassed to admit it was Lee's comments about my teeth and my nose that had really put me off. And the surprise of it, too, of course. Why would he be pretending to be something he wasn't?

"Boy, girl," Hugh went on, "he's still a nice kid."

"He's not *honest!*"

Dad wrinkled his brows at me. I knew that look — a caution not to sound quite so holier-than-thou.

"Wowsy," Hugh said, "it's gonna be hard saying *she* from now on, isn't it?"

"But how can you be so sure, Janet?" Mother asked. "Having pierced ears isn't iron-clad proof, is it, dear? Perhaps in China . . ."

Dad remarked, "Kevin, you've been near the child the most. Did you never notice that he might be . . . ?"

"I never gave it a thought! I'm trying to think . . . You know, it's true, I haven't seen him naked. I go for my shower, and he's dressed by the time I get back. He doesn't shower in the morning, always before bedtime. And he's never at the latrine the same time I am, come to think of it."

"But why the subterfuge?" Dad said with a puzzled look. "I agree with you, Janet, it is rather strange."

"I don't think Mr. Huang is his real uncle, either," I said. "He doesn't look anything like him. I think Lee calls him uncle, just being polite, like we called Mrs. Downing 'Auntie,' 'cuz she was your friend, Mother. And Lee said Dao-Zeun isn't related to either of them!"

"Perhaps that explains it," Mother said. "For some reason or other, Lee needs to travel to the United States, and had no one to go with except a couple of Chinese friends, both of whom are men, so . . ."

"And since she's a girl," Kevin took up the thought, "and not even related, people might have frowned on that arrangement. And now I'm the third man in there with her! Hmm. I'll have to be careful about not dressing in front of *her,* either!"

"We're jumping a bit to conclusions, don't you think?" Hugh said. "And I really don't see what the fuss is."

"Propriety, Hugh," Dad said.

"But you're all making it sound like something *shameful* or . . . something."

"Well, it *is* a mystery!" I said hotly. "You've gotta admit that!"

Hugh refused to get excited about it. He stirred the peas and carrots on his plate into the mashed potatoes and said around a mouthful, "There must be a good explanation."

"Obviously!" I rejoined with my newly acquired tone of sarcasm. At times I found Hugh irritating.

"Well, I'll ask him, her, about it sometime," he said agreeably.

"Don't you *dare!* Lee's *my* friend, and this is *my* mystery!"

"You sounded so mad, I thought he wasn't your friend anymore," Hugh goaded me.

"Not right *now,* he isn't," I said, "but that doesn't mean I can't get back to it."

Mother said firmly, "Before you do, Janet, I suggest you calm down a bit. It's hard to be friends with someone who's as touchy as you've been today."

Kevin flashed his crooked grin at me. In his dark blue eyes I saw his It's-okay-baby-sister look of warmth and empathy, which made me feel better.

But then he said, "I guess it must be the curse of having a tenth birthday coming up soon."

That set me back again. I didn't appreciate it that he called it a curse. But, I thought, at least he's thinking about my birthday.

And then suddenly I guessed that whatever it was he was making in the workshop, it was something for *me!*

# Six

Dad's piece of writing for the Personal Page appeared in the next day's newspaper, and after lunch I lay on my bunk to read it.

At the top of the first column I saw A LESSON by Samuel Baylor, M.D. He always signed himself that way; he was proud of that M.D. after his name. I found the title uninspiring; when people are reading for pleasure, they don't want a lesson. But I had to read it because my dad wrote it.

The other night my younger son asked me if our family's seven years in India had been good ones, and I responded without taking into account what these past years might have meant to my wife and our three children. Were each of us to answer that question, no doubt the answer would be as singularly different as our individual personalities are.

As my response to my son was of a personal nature, so shall these next thoughts be.

To a certain extent, yes, the years were good ones.

If I were to die tomorrow, I trust the Lord would say to me, "Well done, thou good and faithful servant!" (I would very much like that to be written on my tombstone someday.) I have labored hard in His vineyards of diseased fruit. It is a matter of recorded fact that I have treated tens of thousands of out-patients and have performed thousands of surgical procedures. But always I made it clear to each of my patients that my reason for being there was not so much to heal their bodies as to win their souls for my Lord, Jesus Christ. Alas, in comparison to hospital records, the Taxila church's register of converts over the years scarcely covers one page.

But it occurs to me now that in seven long years, my own soul made little contact with any other. I came to know only two Indians as friends to my heart.

And both of them are now lost to me.

The first, Dr. Agarwal, was raised a Hindu, but, on being converted during his years in a Christian medical college, became a devout believer. He became an excellent physician, too. He was a joy to work and converse with. I found in him a kindred spirit. But within three years of his joining my staff at Taxila Christian Hospital he became ill with tuberculosis, and not all of our combined knowledge nor our medicines were able to save him.

That was a loss of a friend to death, but he lives in my heart. The second friend is alive but gone from my life because I broke his heart.

Fear not, I shall be brief in my confession.

His name is Patras (Peter, the rock), but his father did not take the name from the New Testament, as he was a Hindu, and Patras was raised as such, although when I knew him he evidenced great interest in Christianity.

He was one of two young men whom I trained as my surgical assistants. The second young man, Gabriel, was a baptized Christian. Both men were intelligent, hard-working, and seemed trustworthy, but there was something in Patras's cheerful nature that I found the more appealing, perhaps because I spent many more hours in his company than I did in Gabriel's. Patras and I talked a great deal about religion, for instance, and sent many a swift shuttlecock over the net in steamy combats of badminton.

Gradually, both young men assumed additional responsibilities in the hospital's administrative affairs. The yearly audit for Mission Headquarters, however, was one of my duties, and it came to my attention that there was a steady drain of linens, equipment, and pharmaceuticals that could not be accounted for within the bounds of normal attrition and consumption of such materials.

I called each of the young men into my office for private talks regarding the matter. Both were aghast; both paled at the implication that their integrity had been put into question; neither could offer an explanation.

I was already in bed the night of the interrogations when Gabriel came to the door of our bungalow and requested a word with me. We strolled together in the rose garden, and he told me that Patras was the one who was at fault. He said Patras had Hindu middlemen in town who received the stolen goods and medicines and peddled them in the very active black market, of which I was aware, given the fact that British liquor, cigarettes, and weapons of all sorts were readily accessible in the Taxila bazaar, if one so desired such commodities.

Gabriel told me he could produce witnesses — Hindu men who would testify to having made purchases of our hospital's goods from Patras.

And now a curious thing happened in my soul of souls. It was the word *Hindu* that tipped the scales of my willingness to believe one young man over the other. I had labored hard and long to win Patras's soul, but he had proved to be resistant. I thought to myself, Ah, he has been merely toying with me to keep me off guard. He has courted my friendship to blinker my eyes to what he's really up to!

During the following week Gabriel did indeed produce Hindu witnesses to support his accusation of Patras, and I believed every one of them, thinking each to be honorable in his willingness to appear in court, if necessary. It did not occur to me that the few British courts in the Northwest Frontier Province had more serious matters to consider than the disappearance of sheets and blankets, bedpans, bottles of sulfa, and a few vials of morphine.

Our small community, however, buzzed with the

scandal, which prompted the local police to arrest Patras, placing him in Taxila's squalid jailhouse. Patras continued to protest his innocence, which merely led me to believe him a most cunning liar.

Such is the danger of setting one's mind and heart in stony compliance with a preconceived notion and deep-seated prejudice.

Yes, I was wrong in my judgment of both young men — oh, so bitterly wrong! It eventually came to light that it was, in fact, the Christian in our midst who was the thief — a conniving young devil with the name and guileless face of an angel. In addition, it was revealed that Gabriel had used hospital funds with which he had bribed his Hindu informants, compounding his felony.

I went in joy to the jail to witness Patras's release.

He spat in the dust at my feet. Then he walked away, and to this day I have no idea where he is, but I strongly suspect he is not lingering at the door of a church.


I laid the newspaper on my stomach and stared up at the bottom of Hugh's bunk above me.

The story was new to me. No one had ever told me this. I doubted that Kevin and Hugh knew of it, either. It must have happened while we were away at boarding school. I pictured my parents sitting on the verandah during their evenings alone, discussing the situation at length together as it evolved and unfolded and collapsed.

I felt a great surge of love for my father. He did need friends, after all, and he felt pangs in his heart, just as I did.

I felt sorry, for instance, that I'd made Lee run away, and yet I couldn't bring myself to say so, not until she made the first move and came to me to explain why she was pretending to be a boy.

My brothers, on reading Dad's "confession," reacted quite differently. Kevin said, "You notice how he managed to praise himself as an excellent doctor?" and Hugh said, "Yeah, but we knew that part. What surprised me was that Dad admitted he'd made a mistake. It makes me feel a whole lot better to know he's not perfect."

"Huh," Kevin grunted, "that's what I've been trying to tell you all along."

One very hot night, the five of us in the family spread our blankets on deck and looked at the stars in the velvety sky. The ship rocked so steeply from side to side, we had to put out our hands and feet and brace ourselves against one another to keep from sliding. But other than that it was peaceful and utterly quiet except for the rhythmic whooshing of the water as the ship pushed its way along.

Kevin said into the darkness, "We're zigzagging again tonight. If you keep your eye on a certain star long enough, you'll see we're not going in a straight line."

"Mike said that's to make it harder for torpedoes to hit us," Hugh said.

"Oh please, not that again!" Mother said with a sigh.

Kevin sighed back at her. "Not mentioning it, Mother, doesn't make it any less a possibility."

He was lying on the blanket beside me, and now he squirmed from one elbow to another.

"And I'll tell you something else. After crossing the Equator, you'd have thought we'd be veering east by now, but we're not, we're headed due south. More like southeast, maybe. I'll bet we're headed for Australia."

Mother sat up. "Australia! Good heavens!"

"Yup, speaking of which . . ." Kevin continued, flopping over on his back now and pointing to a cluster of stars, "there's the Southern Cross. See it? Just ignore the fifth little one, and you'll see the big four others make a perfect cross. See it?"

We all murmured uh-huh.

"That same formation is on the flags of four countries. Did you know that?"

"No," I said. "How do you know that?"

"I don't know how, I just do. Once I must've noticed those four associated themselves with this particular constellation. Things like that interest me, I guess."

"Which four?" Hugh asked from where he lay on the other side of Dad, and it occurred to me that it was unusual for Dad to remain so quiet. Ordinarily it was he who told us this kind of tidbit that seemed to me quite unnecessary to know.

Kevin said the four were Australia, New Zealand, Western Samoa, and Papua New Guinea.

"I don't know where that last place is," Hugh said.

Dad spoke up. "If we traveled north of Australia, going east toward California, we'd pass right below it, after Java. But it would be far too dangerous to be anywhere near there right now. We have no choice but to circle south of Australia and angle our way up through the Pacific from there."

"You've known this all along, haven't you, Sam?" Mother asked, sounding a bit peeved.

"Not all along, but . . ."

"It's got something to do with the captain's secret, huh?" Hush asked excitedly.

"Yes," Dad replied quietly. "I can tell you now that we're going to be stopping at Melbourne, and when we get there, you'll see why."

Sometimes I had to admire his restraint. He was so good at keeping other people's secrets he didn't even let Mother in on them.

# Seven

On the morning of our seventeenth day at sea, I awoke with my arm hanging out over the edge of the bunk, and when I tried to raise it, it felt like lead, not part of my body. Using my other hand to lift the dead arm into bed with me, I lay still while it pingled back to life.

But that wasn't what had awakened me. It was something else. What?

The ship's engines had turned off, that was it! It was terribly quiet all around me.

I climbed up to Hugh's bunk. "We're here!" I whispered. "It's Australia! Let's go!"

Dad said firmly from his bunk, "You kids stay right where you are. It's not quite time to get up yet."

"But Dad! I want to see a koala and a kangaroo!"

"They'll wait for you, Janet. Go back to sleep a while."

That was impossible. I lay awake thinking about meeting an aborigine. And I wanted to see a duck-billed platypus. In our geography class at school we'd seen pictures of all the strange creatures of this continent where God had let His imagination run wild during the Creation.

I was full of excitement as I dressed. If this is a harbor, I thought, there must be a beach, too. But we wouldn't swim far out because I'd heard there were sharks here like nobody's business.

Mother said happily, "Won't it be lovely to stretch our legs on shore!"

"I'd like to buy a boomerang," Hugh said.

We headed up to breakfast with our hats on, and Mother carried her purse.

The S.P. in the gangway held up a hand. "Looks like you folks are thinking of going ashore, but you may as well forget it."

"Why?" I screeched.

"Captain's orders, Miss."

"But *why?*"

"Captain's orders," he repeated. "No civilians allowed off the ship."

Oh, it was cruel! And no explanation for it!

Dad said, "I trust we may go up on deck?"

"Oh yes, you and your family may be on deck as much as you like, long as we're anchored here. No problem with that."

Only on deck! To be able to see land and not walk on it? Beaches and not go swimming? Did they think, if we left, we wouldn't come back? We would be leaving our steamers behind as proof of our intention to return. And we didn't know any military secrets we could tell anybody. Well, Dad did, but he'd said that one would be solved once we got here, so what else were they worried about?

Hugh said disconsolately, "Paolo gets to go ashore, but he's not happy about it. He said he and the other prisoners are being kicked off here. He was hoping to go to California."

We delayed going to breakfast and climbed our way up the ladders to the deck.

"There's your answer," Dad said soberly, nodding down at the dock below us.

A long line of Red Cross ambulances as well as trucks with the cross painted on them stood with their engines idling as military medical personnel and some of our ship's crew members were removing stretchers with men on them and were then hurrying to carry them up our gangplank.

"American G.I.s, mostly," Dad told us, his voice heavy with emotion. "A number of Navy men, too. And some British. All of them wounded. A few of them are also seriously ill with tropical diseases. Brought here from all over the Pacific Theater of war. Captain Jackson said there are, at last count, nine hundred and fifty-six of them."

"Why British, too?" Hugh asked.

"My guess is the hospitals here and in Sydney are crowded these days. London's, too. Many of these men will need prostheses." Dad caught my quizzical look and added, "Artificial arms and legs. Requiring long periods of therapy."

For quite some time none of us spoke. We stared down at the young men on the stretchers. Once in a while one of them would look up at us and wave a bit.

Kevin joined us at the railing. He'd missed us at breakfast, he said. Then he too looked down and stood there speechless.

Finally Mother said, "It breaks my heart — "

Dad put an arm around her. "This will take a while. *Days,* I suspect. I could use a cup of coffee. How about you, Nellie?"

Being away from the immediate scene loosened our tongues. How long had the wounded men waited for our ship? Would any of them die before we got them safely to America? Meanwhile, where would we put them all?

Dad didn't have all the answers, but he did tell us the casualty cases were being put into the hold of the ship.

"The hold!" Mother exclaimed, her face looking aghast.

Yes, Dad said, the captain had taken him down there. They'd made a temporary hospital of it, a most unusual hospital because most of the beds were hammocks, strung one above the other.

Hammocks! I thought. What about those who were

in the top hammocks when an alarm went off? And what would it be like to be in a hammock, anyway, day after day, and not feeling well? Hammocks were fun for a while, but no one would want to spend days and nights in one. You couldn't roll over. Your back needed a straight place. Lying out on the hard deck would be better. But there wasn't enough room on the decks to have hundreds of people stretched out. And, anyway, there were storms, and then what?

I heard Kevin say, "So the captain wants you to help out, huh, Dad?"

"A number of military doctors and nurses are coming aboard," Dad said, "but, yes, they'll need all the help they can get."

"But why was this all such a big secret?" Hugh wanted to know, and I was glad he'd asked it.

"Everything having to do with this ship — its movements, its list of troop-class passengers, its cargo — all of that is Confidential and Classified information, Hugh. Imagine if the Japanese were to know . . ."

"But these guys are wounded, Dad!" Hugh objected. "No threat to anyone!"

"I imagine Captain Jackson is particularly interested in keeping that fact a secret, don't you see? In the event of an attack on us, able-bodied men would stand a better chance of surviving."

"Oh," Hugh said, pushing an uneaten sausage aside.

After breakfast, we went up to the deck again. Without the breeze of the moving ship, it was very hot already in the mid-morning sun, as this was Australia's summer season, and many of the civilians who crowded at the railing wore sunbonnets or pith helmets. Everyone was looking down at the continual line of stretchers that were being carried up the gangplank.

The S.P.s told us we had to stay out of the way, but after a while my brothers and I edged our way to the top of the gangplank so we could greet the wounded men as they arrived, and no one shooed us away.

"Hello!" Hugh was the first to say to a man who appeared to be our father's age. He had a sunburned nose and cheeks that needed a shave. His eyes were bright and friendly.

"A pleasure to see you, boy!" he said to Hugh. "Take it easy, you hear?"

"You too!"

As the sailors carried him past us, I saw that the sheet which covered him stopped strangely short. He was missing both legs!

Now here came a younger man, with dark curly hair and a very thin face. His eyes were closed. His sheet covered him from chin to toes, I saw, but it seemed to me the bulk of his person under it was less than Hugh's ever looked under his!

I leaned down and said, "Hi! You're going to be okay now!"

He opened his eyes and whispered, "That's fine. Thank you, that's fine to know."

The next man had his entire head wrapped in bandages, with only a hole that exposed the tip of his nose and his mouth. His lips were chapped, I noticed. A Navy nurse, holding up a bottle of plasma with a tube running down, walked beside his stretcher. From under her peaked white cap her yellow hair hung in dark sweaty strands. She shook her head at us, but Hugh said, "Hi, Sir!" and reached out to touch the man's arm. He got no response.

I said to the nurse, "You should put salve on his lips," but she only looked at me disapprovingly.

The following young soldier was holding up his own bottle of a clear liquid. He had a tattoo of a scorpion on his forearm. His chin was firmly set and his eyes were squinting hard, as though he were bracing himself against pain. When he saw Kevin, his eyes opened wider and seemed to blaze with fury.

"You're bloody . . . next!" he said, the first two words said firmly, his voice breaking on the third.

Kevin nodded at him, and I guessed he'd been thinking that very same thought.

Another man, this one with a full beard, moved an arm without a hand at the end of it, and said to Kevin, "I hope this conflict will be over before it's your turn, son!"

We greeted each man as he was carried on board.

One by one. Hour after hour. Some of them seemed happy to see us:

"Thanks!"

"Hi to you, too!"

"Thanks, Miss! I feel safer now, knowing you're on board!"

"Good to see ya, kid."

"Thank God!"

"American kids! Whaddaya know!"

Others responded listlessly:

"Yeah."

"Sure."

"Okay."

And many were incapable of saying a word.

Mother came to get us at lunchtime.

"That's enough for one morning, I think," she said heavily.

Dad had gone down to the hold, she told us, to assist with the soldiers' hammock assignments, and we didn't see him again until suppertime, when he came up for a quick bite.

He had been working all day, he said, with a young Navy doctor who was grateful for his assistance and judgment based on many years of experience. The decisions regarding the placement of the men were made according to the amount of care each one would require, such as for those who were unconscious or incapable of feeding themselves. But some of the lower hammocks had also been given to the men who suffered a disease like typhoid, characterized by frequent vomiting and diarrhea. Then too, there was the psychological factor; a few of the men had refused to be put in a position that would limit their access to freedom in the event of an emergency.

On mentioning this last contingency, Dad closed his eyes and rubbed the back of his neck. "It would be chaos," he whispered. "They would be doomed."

He took a deep breath. "We're swamped with work."

"Can't I be of some help, Sam?" Mother asked.

"No, Nellie, I don't want you down there. It isn't a place . . ." He paused, shaking his head. "I want you to rest, Nell."

"But *I* could help!" Kevin said. "I can hold the basins while they're vomiting, Dad," he proposed, his face so full of enthusiasm one might have imagined such a thing would be pleasant to do. "I can empty bedpans! Or shave the guys who can't do it themselves. Okay?"

Dad looked away. At length he said quietly, "I'll talk with the Chief Medical Officer and see what he thinks about that, Son. If he agrees, I think it would be a good thing for you to do. And I certainly would be pleased to have you down there with me."

Hugh exclaimed, "How about me? I could help, too!"

"And me!" I chimed in.

Dad regarded us with stern looks. "You two children are never to come down there, do you hear? Never!"

"Not fair," Hugh muttered, putting on his black-sheep look, but I felt relieved; emptying bedpans didn't sound like a lot of fun.

The next day Mother had a migraine headache as well as a recurrence of her dysentery. She looked miserable. She lay on her bunk with a cool cloth on her head and kept throwing it aside to make her frequent trips down the gangway.

Hugh and I stayed with her in the cabin until at last she drifted off in a snooze. Then we went to watch the stretcher procession again, but this time we didn't stand at the head of the gangplank. It was too depressing.

Lee came to stand beside us. I hadn't seen her since the day I'd guessed she wasn't a boy, so I still hadn't heard her admit it.

I saw immediately that she was holding a stuffed toy koala. I hardly looked at Lee; I had eyes only for that koala. I was terribly envious.

I didn't even say hello. I said, "Where'd you get that?"

She glanced over her shoulder at Mr. Huang, who was standing a few feet away. "Uncle had a sailor buy it."

"Can I hold it a minute?"

Lee handed it over.

The koala had an adorable face, with black button eyes, a black leather nose, and little ears that stood at attention. Its stubby legs had jagged pieces of leather sewn on at the ends to suggest tiny paws. Its fur was blackish brown and so wonderfully soft I had to give it a hug.

Hugh reached out to stroke it. "That's rabbit fur, " he pronounced. "That wasn't a real koala, thank goodness. They've just made it to look like one."

"Cute, though," I said. "I want one. How can I get one?"

"We'll ask Mike," Hugh said. "The sailors are allowed to go ashore. Mike'll get you one."

"They cost a lot," Lee said.

"Well, in that case . . ." Hugh mumbled.

"*We've* got money!" I protested.

"Not much," Hugh said. "Not enough if it cost *lots.*"

"It's my birthday, day after tomorrow," I reminded him, "and that's what I *want!*"

"You can't always get what you want, Jannie. Heck, on my birthday all I got was another jackknife."

I turned to Lee. "Ask your uncle how much it costs, and we'll see."

Lee took her koala back and held it possessively to her chest.

"What're we supposed to call you now, anyway," I said abruptly, "now that you've turned into a girl."

"You can call me Lily," she said softly, pronouncing the *i* as a long *e*.

I was full of antagonism for those beautiful dark eyes that suddenly took on a scared-rabbity look.

"What do you mean 'call' you? Is that your name or isn't it?" I said sharply.

"It's Lily."

"Well, why didn't you say so in the first place?"

"Reasons."

"Like what sort of reasons?"

"Take it easy, Jannie," Hugh put in.

Lily seemed encouraged by this note of caution and support. She said with more strength in her voice, "Please, you can go on calling me Lee. It's half of Lily, you see?"

"And you'd rather not have anyone else know about it, is that it?" Hugh asked.

She gave him a dazzling smile. "That's it!"

Hugh nodded. "I guess we could help you out there, if that's what you want." He glanced at me to see what I thought.

"I suppose so," I reluctantly agreed, "but you gotta tell us *why* by the time we get to California!"

Lee shook her head. She said she couldn't promise to tell us by then, but if we would give her our address in the States, she would write us a letter about it once the war was over.

I wasn't at all happy with this proposal, but Lee was

stubborn, so I was left with two choices: Be stubborn, too, and *never* find out the answer or let her be my friend again.

As to owning a stuffed koala all my own, Dad said that was out of the question. Hugh wasn't going to get a boomerang, either. Koalas cost twenty dollars and boomerangs cost ten, and Dad had only a few hundred dollars set aside, he said, to get our family to Michigan, put down-payments on a house and a car, and set up a medical practice of his own. We were not "in the chips" enough to be able to afford luxuries.

I was in the dumps about it for a full day. (Also, I was developing another of my boils just then, so I had plenty of excuses to feel sorry for myself.) I saw sailors return from their shore leave with koalas under their arms, presumably for a daughter or a sister back home, and I resented having a father who was poorer than a sailor. In addition, the sailors appeared to have had a very good time, laughing a lot, some of them so tipsy they needed to lean on their friends; whereas we passengers were stuck on board, and I, for one, was beginning to find it tiresome watching people being carried on stretchers.

Hugh, Lee, and I finally gave up on it. We had the deck to ourselves, except for Mr. Huang and a few others who sat in shady spots to read. We kids drew chalk-lines to play hopscotch and a game Lee taught us, called Minotaur, which meant drawing complicated mazes. I gave no thought whatsoever to my mother in bed or to my father and Kevin working down in the hold.

But at mealtimes, Mother joined Hugh and me in the mess, if only to have a cup of tea and a cracker or two, and if Dad and Kevin could make it, the three of us bombarded them with questions: What was it like down there? Was it terribly hot? Was there lots of moaning and groaning? Was it stinky with vomit and so forth? How were the bottles of plasma held up? Were the nurses terribly busy? Where had the man with no legs been put? And the one with his head wrapped in bandages? How did the men get up into or out of their hammocks? How, in general, were their spirits? They were happy, no doubt, to be going home, but were they anxious about being in the hold? Were they afraid?

Neither Dad nor Kevin seemed eager to talk about it. They both stared into their bowls of soup and gave irritatingly cryptic answers: Yes, it was hot . . . and stinky . . . there were I.V. poles . . . nurses were assigned to total-care patients . . . there were ladders. Apropos of the last question, Dad said the ship's chaplain had asked the Reverend James Foster to come down and give support where he could. There was also a priest. And a rabbi.

Dad laid down his spoon and rested his bristly chin on his fists. "Captain Jackson tells us it will be another three weeks before we get to California."

"Three weeks!" Mother exclaimed wearily.

"He'll need to keep zigzagging, Nellie, especially as we pass by the Pacific Islands. Yes, he estimates three more weeks. But if all goes well, I think we'll lose only ten or twelve of the men down there."

"Only . . . Oh dear! Do you think Kevin should — "

"Kevin's been a brick," Dad said warmly, "an absolute brick. We could use ten more like him."

At that moment I felt I would gladly have given up possessing any number of koalas to have my father say something like that about me.

Meanwhile, the stretchers kept coming, as well as new loads of stores and baggage, fuel oil, diesel oil, and fresh water.

After supper on our third day of being moored at Princess Pier in Melbourne's harbor, Dad said he and Kevin were taking a break from their duties in the hold, and we all went down to C23 for our family's evening prayers.

Dad had just opened the Bible when a knock came on the door, and there was Mike Turner with a big grin on his face and something so enormous stuffed under his uniform, he looked pregnant. He was supporting the bulge with his left hand, and in the other he held a number of cereal bowls and soup spoons.

"Say, folks, I hope I'm not disturbin' nothin', but I got us a treat here. Australian ice cream. The best in the world. Even better than we got in the States."

He unveiled a sturdy container, and since there wasn't a table in our cabin, he set it down on the floor.

"A whole gallon, just for us!" he announced happily. "And bowls here to go with it."

Dad started to say in an amazed tone, "Where'd you get . . ."

"You don't want to ask that, Sir."

"But . . ."

"Sometimes as this sort of stuff is gettin' loaded on board, one or two of the items gets lost in the shuffle, you know?" He glanced delightedly into each of our faces.

"You *took* it, didn't you, Mike?" Dad asked sternly.

"Oh, now, well . . . you wouldn't want to say I exactly *took* it," Mike said, "'cause as I was helpin' to load these things into the freezer, this particular one was just sittin' there, gettin' ready to melt, and you wouldn't want that, would you? If I was to take it back now, all the way up there, it'd be so ruint I'd have to chuck it overboard, and you tell me what's the point in that?"

To my great relief, Dad smiled and said, "I agree, no point in that."

So we all dug in. It was the best, richest ice cream I'd ever had in my life, and obviously Dad thought so, too, because he had three bowlsful.

When we six had emptied the gallon container, Dad said to Mike, "Just as you came, we were about to have our family prayers. Would you like to stay and join in with us?"

"That I would," he replied simply.

"We're making our way through the Psalms this month, reading two or three a night," Dad told him, "and tonight it's my wife's turn to read."

He handed the Bible to Mother, and she began to read in the loving tones she always gave to her reading of the Bible or when she prayed aloud, her spirit apparently in perfect accord with the words she read or said. Her voice in those moments was especially soothing to me.

"Psalm 64. 'Hear my voice, O God, in my complaint . . .'" she began and glanced up at Dad before she continued:

> " 'preserve my life from dread of the enemy;
> hide me from the secret plots of the wicked,
> from the scheming of evildoers,
> who whet their tongues like swords,
> who aim bitter words like arrows,
> shooting from ambush at the blameless,
> shooting at him suddenly . . .'"

Mother laid the Bible down. "Oh, Samuel, I'm sorry, but I can't go on with this one! I think we need to be thinking about lifting up our hearts, not about enemies lying in ambush."

Dad reached for the Bible. "I'll finish reading, then,"

he said stiffly, giving Mother a look much like he gave one of us kids when we were being difficult.

"Dr. Baylor, Sir," Mike spoke up, "if you was to turn ahead to a hunnerd and twenty-one, all our hearts would be gentled."

Dad looked up at him in some surprise. I was surprised, too, both at the interruption and the mention of a number I didn't know off hand.

"Yes, all right," Dad said, turning the pages.

He began to read:

> " *'I will lift up mine eyes unto the hills.*
> *From whence cometh my help?*
> *My help cometh from the Lord,*
> *Who hath made heaven and earth . . .'* "

Later that evening, two young Australian women with two children, a toddler and a baby, came on board and moved into the cabin across the way from ours. One of the young women, who introduced herself simply as Lorraine, was very pretty, her blond hair short and curly, but I thought her lipstick was too dark. The toddler was her child, a sweet-faced three-year-old named Dawn. The second woman, Dorothy, holding baby John, was coarse-looking, I thought. She had red hair, but an inch of black roots was showing, and she'd plucked her eyebrows and had drawn in other ones with their ends sweeping up. Her eyes weren't friendly. Her breasts in a black brassiere under a see-through blouse jutted out in sharp points, and she wore black mesh stockings under a very short skirt.

As I was looking her up and down, I noticed she was doing the same to Mother and didn't seem to like what she saw.

They told us they were going to the States to live with their husbands, whom they'd married when the men had been stationed temporarily in Melbourne.

Then the two women went into their cabin, closing the door firmly, and went into peals of laughter which we could hear even with our door closed as well.

# Eight

The next morning, which was my birthday, I awoke to the sound of the ship's engines and the familiar sensation of the ship's rolling.

We were on our way again! The breadth of the Pacific Ocean lay ahead of us.

My parents and Hugh gave me Happy Birthday kisses, but there wasn't a present in sight. I did my best to hide my disappointment; I'd thought a person's tenth birthday was a significant one, deserving of a gift or two.

After breakfast Mother told me to go back to the cabin to make up my bunk. Again, I was disappointed; we had a rule in our family that a birthday was a day on which one didn't have to do a lick of work.

Feeling like a martyr, I went to my bunk. And there under the covers was a koala! Oh, what joy!

Mother and Dad were full of grins. So was Hugh, and especially so when he was given a non-birthday present — the boomerang he'd wanted. Kevin was there, looking on as though he were holding his breath. He held a paper bag and now he handed it to me. The bag was heavy. I reached in and withdrew a two-toned wooden box, shorter than a shoebox but higher, its varnished finish very glossy and smooth to the touch. On the lid was a painting of Bambi, exactly like Walt Disney's, and the lid was held closed with a shiny little brass catch.

"I made it for you," Kevin said, his eyes bright with pride.

"You *made* it! For *me?*" I was moved to think he had gone to such effort, and, on examining the box more closely, I was impressed by the workmanship; but it was Dad who, in taking the box into his own hands, helped me see how truly fine it was by pointing out how perfectly the light and dark strips of wood had been aligned and how neat the edges were.

"It's a fine piece of work," Dad said to Kevin. "Your grandfather will be proud of you when he sees it." (Dad's father was a cabinetmaker.)

Now Hugh dug into his pants pocket and held out to me something enclosed in his fist.

"And I made *this* for you," he said, looking very pleased with himself. He turned his fist over and opened it.

On his palm lay a tiny hippopotamus, carved in dark wood.

"Paolo showed me how to make it," Hugh said happily. "I worked a long time on getting it just right and sanding it down."

I picked it up. It was about three inches long — a hippo in a lying-down position, with its belly bulging out at the sides, its eyes closed, and a peaceful smile on its fat face.

"Oh . . . !" was all I could say at the moment, wishing he had chosen a different animal. But the more I looked at it, the better I liked it, and I could see that a lot of effort and love had gone into the making of this carving, as had been true in the construction of the Bambi box.

Mother held out a hand, and I let her hold the little hippo. She turned it around and around in her slim hands, examining its face, its backside, its underside, and then looking at its sleepy face again before she gave it a quick kiss and handed it back to me.

"It's lovely, Hugh," she said. "Really lovely."

"Yes, thank you so much!" I exclaimed. "Thank you, everyone! Kevin and Hugh and Mother and Dad! This is my best birthday ever!"

And it wasn't over.

Mike came with an entire box of Hershey bars, which, Dad said, I could either share with the family or consume by myself at the rate of only half a bar a day.

So we all had one, and there were plenty left.

Mike then laid on Mother's lap a small package

wrapped in pink paper. "And this is for the special lady who's the mother of this dear girl."

"Oh, Mike . . . oh, my goodness . . . what . . . ?"

She unwrapped it, being careful not to tear the paper, as though she were hoping to save it to use again someday.

It was a little oblong box. I had no idea what it was, but Mother's eyes glistened with pleasure as she opened it and took out a narrow bottle with a gold-colored cap.

"Chanel Number Five!" she exclaimed in delight. "Well . . . I never . . . ! But . . . you shouldn't have! Oh my!"

We were all terribly pleased to see how happy she was, and Mike looked especially so.

At lunchtime, Mrs. Dobson brought her dessert and coffee over to our table and asked if she could join us. Mother greeted her a bit coolly, I thought, although she said all the right words and asked Kevin to pull up a chair for the woman.

"Happy Birthday, Janet," Mrs. Dobson said, placing a small package on my lap.

"Thank you! Shall I open it now?"

"If you like."

It was another box, a rectangular silver one, about five inches long, the kind of box a woman might keep bits of jewelry in. On its lid were the figures of a lion and a sheep lying next to each other, and I saw they'd been molded, not just etched. It was very pretty, but not the sort of thing I would have picked out for myself. Nevertheless, I thanked her profusely.

Mother asked to take a closer look at it, and when she did so, she looked astounded. "But . . . Mrs. Dobson! This is *sterling* silver! This must be an heirloom!"

Ann Dobson nodded and smiled.

"But you mustn't give such a valuable thing to a child!"

"I want her to have it," she replied firmly. "I would like her to remember me by it."

I promised I would, and thanked her all over again.

Mrs. Dobson turned to my father. "Dr. Baylor, I understand you and your son are working with the wounded. I would like very much to offer my assistance. I've had a good deal of experience with those who are ill, and you, in turn, would be doing me a great favor, as I'm finding the time hanging heavy on me."

Dad was shaking his head. "First of all, it's not my decision to make. And, I must tell you, it's an awful environment for a woman. My wife volunteered to help, but frankly I'm glad she isn't there, particularly since she herself is not feeling well."

"I understand that," Mrs. Dobson said with a sympathetic nod. "It's important she rests. I am fortunate to be in good health, and I can't tell you how much I would welcome some work to do."

Dad said cautiously, "Even the qualified nurses who are there are finding it very difficult, I think."

Mrs. Dobson was not deterred by this. "I ask only that you put in a good word for me," she said, giving my father a beautiful smile. "It's possible I could simply help at mealtimes when some of the men might appreciate someone to talk with."

I saw that Mother was not taking kindly to this suggestion, but Kevin looked pleased with the prospect of her being there.

Dad said solemnly, "I'll see what I can do, Mrs. Dobson. I'll have a word with the Chief Medical Officer, if that's what you'd like."

"Oh, I would, indeed! Thank you so much!" She rose from the table, touched me briefly on the shoulder, and left us.

At that moment, as though they had been waiting for Mrs. Dobson to leave, the Rev. and Mrs. Foster came to our table and handed me something soft, wrapped in that morning's newspaper.

I thanked them and unceremoniously tore the package open. (Years later I wished I had saved that paper with my birthdate on it.) Inside was a folded piece of cloth. It was of fine red wool, intricately embroidered. I lifted it up and held it out. It was the kind of shawl an old woman might drape around her shoulders or the kind of thing someone might want to hang on a wall.

"But that's a *Pashmina!*" Mother exclaimed, putting a hand to her mouth in amazement.

"Oh, no, you *mustn't!*" Dad said to the Fosters.

I looked from one adult face to another, trying to assess my parents' outbursts of protest and the Fosters' expressions of pleasure over having given me such a gift.

"We want you to have it," Mrs. Foster said, more to Mother and Dad than to me. "We were able to purchase more than one, and it would please us to know Janet has it. Someday when she looks back on her early years in India, she'll treasure it."

I realized with chagrin that she had noticed I was not terribly thrilled with the shawl at that moment.

Later Hugh said, "You didn't thank them enough, Jannie. That shawl's worth at least fifty stuffed koalas. Maybe even two hundred. Look at the *work* that went into it!"

Together we examined the thousands of tiny embroidered stitches that covered every inch of the woolen cloth, and I suddenly felt it a great burden to possess a thing of such value.

And still my day of surprises was not over! Captain Jackson invited me and my brothers to his quarters "for a bit of birthday cake at 1600 hrs.," as his handwritten note informed us.

I put on my Sunday cotton dress. Kevin and Hugh wore their best shorts and short-sleeved white shirts. Nevertheless, the three of us felt hot and sweaty as we climbed up the ladders.

When we arrived, an ordinary seaman let us in, immediately conveying the captain's regrets that he could not be there, after all, as something urgent had called him away, but we were to enjoy the cake and ice cream, nonetheless.

In disappointed silence, we sat in a gingerly fashion on the sofas in the room that was in great contrast to our cabin. It was bright with sunlight, for one thing, with three portholes thrown open, reducing the heat not one whit, however. On the walls were photos and colorful maps, and on the floor was an oriental rug, predominantly blue. In one corner of the room was a highly polished copper table with cut-glass decanters on it.

The sailor had left the room. My brothers and I rolled our eyes at each other, saying nothing.

There was a knock at the door. Mr. Huang was there to deliver Lee! She looked around, handed me a package, saying, "Happy Birthday!" and sat down without another word.

Lee had made me a new macramé elf's pot holder, this one having been constructed from twine. I gave her a hug.

Then here came Lorraine, to drop off her little girl, Dawn, who looked quite terrified when her mother left her at the door.

The sailor returned, bearing a giant cake with yellow roses on it, made very cleverly of frosting.

"Compliments of the chef, Miss," he said, handing me a long knife with which to cut it.

Although I thought it a strange party, I was impressed by the fact that both the captain and the chef had taken such special notice of me.

Anxious to leave, we hurried to eat our portions of cake and our bowls of melting ice cream. All of us, that is, except for little Dawn, who had wrapped her piece of cake in a paper napkin and was stirring her ice cream into soup.

"Eat your cake, Dawn," Kevin said to her. "Eat your yellow rose."

She shook her head, looking very solemn. Her light blue eyes showed no glint of pleasure in them.

"I want to take my cake to my mommy," she said, pronouncing the words "tike" and "kike."

I said quickly, "You can take her as much as you like! But *you* eat some, too!"

For the first time since she'd arrived, her expression relaxed. She unwrapped the piece of cake, took a bite of it, and looked up at me, her face full of rapture. But she wouldn't eat the rose. She wrapped it up again in the napkin, and I wondered what it would look like the next time she unveiled it.

Before we left, we put slices of the cake on three paper plates, for Mother and Dad, Mr. Huang and Dao-Zeun, and Lorraine and Dorothy.

Dawn took my hand as we returned to our cabins. "Thank you for the lovely party," she said, so politely and clearly for such a little one, I thought. Then she added, "I'm going to keep the rose always!"

Before I went to bed that night, I took out my survival kit and dumped its contents on my bed. I made a tight package of my extra pieces of clothing and the rubber poncho and shoved it down to the bottom of the canvas bag. Then I put my two remaining Hershey bars, the small bottles of salt tablets and aspirins, my extra toothbrush and tube of toothpaste, the jar of cold cream and the bar of soap — all of these items I put into my birthday Bambi box, leaving some room at the top. I rolled up the little hippo in one of my dad's cotton handkerchiefs and put it in the silver box, which I laid uppermost, before securing the brass latch. Then I wrapped the wooden box in my extra sweater and jammed it into the bag. Never in my life had I felt such a responsibility to keep treasures safe. I was not altogether happy to have them if it meant worrying so much about them.

And what was I to do with that *Pashmina* shawl?

"*You* put this away somewhere," I said, handing it to Mother. "You like it better anyway."

She gave me a searching look before she reached under her bunk, drew out one of the steamer trunks, and put the shawl in it.

"But it's not safe there!" I pointed out.

"It's as safe as anything can be in this world, Janet," she said with a sad little smile. "I learned . . . let's see, I guess it was about five years ago, I learned not to set my heart on any material possession. And that lesson has given me a great sense of liberty, come to think of it," she added, but I didn't think she sounded entirely convinced.

"Did you lose something precious?" I asked.

"Yes, a Delft vase. I don't suppose you remember it. It was a wedding present from your father's uncle. It was lovely to look at. I packed it more carefully than anything else and brought it to India with us. Then one day when I'd filled it with fresh roses and was reaching up to put it on the mantelpiece, it slipped out of my hands and smashed to smithereens. And I wept. I went to the bedroom and cried about it bitterly."

Mother looked down at her hands and studiously proceeded to push back the cuticle of one fingernail.

"And that day," she went on, "I decided . . . that day I decided never again to set my heart on a mere *thing*. I appreciate beautiful things, as you know, but I can't let myself *love* them."

"I *love* my koala," I said. "If we have to go overboard, he's going right with me, tucked under my safety belt. And I love Hugh's hippo and Kevin's Bambi box. I'm going to keep them forever!"

"It's good that you're so appreciative of your birthday gifts," Mother acknowledged, "but by the time you're my age, you'll be surprised at all the things in your life that you once valued but have had to let go for one reason or another."

I turned away from her. Every once in a while she would say something on the order of "Wait until you're as old as I am . . ." and I didn't find it helpful at all.

# Nine

No doubt there are times in the year when the Pacific Ocean is fairly flat and calm, behaving in a manner consistent with its name, but now in the latter part of January, the world's greatest body of water was angry. Its threatening gestures were expressed in giant, dark-green swells rather than in the sharp, white-capped waves such as I'd seen in pictures of storms on other seas.

It was both thrilling and frightening to stand on the deck and feel oneself plunge with the ship into a deep trough and see the looming emerald mountains of water on either side, and then, at the last minute, it seemed, before the ship was overwhelmed, whoosh! ahh! it would be swiftly lifted up. There one would be again, above it all, riding high, until that supporting swell fell away, hurtling the ship into another valley, with new cliffs rising up on both sides, threatening to engulf the ship as easily as if it were no larger than a canoe.

As we headed eastward, the situation grew worse, with the ship rolling, indeed, "like a pig in a mud-bath," as Mike had said earlier, and we surely did need the guardrails on our bunks to keep from falling out. When we stood at the cabin's little sink to brush our teeth, we were obliged to stand with legs akimbo to keep our balance. When we walked along the gangways, we staggered as though we were drunk.

And then one morning we were told we could no longer go on deck. It was too dangerous. Last night a crew member had been washed overboard!

Later that day, his round, freckled face taut with emotion and his voice occasionally breaking, Mike reported to us, "We threw him a lifesaver, but . . . if he got aholt of it, maybe, but . . . oh, golly . . . God rest his soul. Maybe a local fisherman will find him. Y'understand, Cap'n Jackson can't turn us 'round, and even if he could . . . Well, it don't bear thinkin' 'bout. Y'all keep away from the decks!"

That night, when the four of us were already in our pajamas, we heard crying in Lorraine and Dorothy's cabin nearby. First it was baby John, and then little Dawn began to call out plaintively, "Mommy! Mommy, come back!"

Mother said, her voice full of distress, "Those young women have left their little ones all alone! Where could they be at this hour?"

"I passed 'em in the gangway a while ago, all gussied

up," Hugh said. "They're with a couple of the officers, I bet."

"Oh," Mother said with a frown. She and Dad gave each other significant glances.

"They're *very* young women, Nell," Dad commented, in a rather sympathetic tone, I thought.

"I realize that," Mother responded, "but their first thought should be for their children. And they're *married!*"

We lay in our bunks, but it was impossible to sleep, with the baby screaming now and Dawn beginning to sound quite hysterical.

"I must see what I can do for them," Mother said, putting on her dressing gown. I offered to help, but she said, "No, go to sleep. It's late."

I lay awake listening. Within a minute or so, Dawn had stopped crying, and after another few minutes, the baby was soothed, as well. I wondered how long Mother would remain in there with them, and began to doze off now that it was quiet.

Mother touched my arm. "Janet," she whispered, "let Dawn crawl in with you."

The little girl snuggled next to me. She smelled of soap and baby powder, and went to sleep almost immediately.

I saw that Mother had brought the baby with her, too, and was preparing to take him into her own bunk with her. He was holding his own bottle and looked very peaceful with his eyes closed as he drank.

Dad leaned out of his upper bunk. "All well now, Nellie?"

"Yes," she whispered. "The baby was slammed up against his railing. And a dirty diaper. Both of them hot and uncomfortable. Gave them sponge baths. Found a clean bottle. Some cans of milk. I've left the mothers a note."

She turned out the light, and we all went to sleep.

I awoke to the sound of harsh whispers:

"... *dare* you bring them ...!"

"... *dare* you leave them ...!"

"... poke your nose into ...!"

"... *reek* of alcohol!"

"... your *business* anyway!"

"... your *first* responsibility ...!"

"Can't *expect* us to ... and *boring!*"

"... *children* with children!"

Dad sat up in his bunk and said sternly, "Young ladies, it's almost four in the morning! You have no sense of time nor proper conduct. And *certainly* no manners! Take your babies with you. Good *night!*"

At breakfast the next morning, Lorraine stopped at our table to thank Mother. "Don't mind Dorothy," she added. "She forgets her manners when she's had too much to drink. As for me, I just *knew* you would look after our kittens."

Mother frowned at the word "kittens" but didn't comment on it. Instead she said, "Neighbors are often helpful, but you can't go through life counting on them. Dawn needed *you* last night. I wonder if you know how much she loves you. She couldn't stop talking about you — 'My mommy' this, and 'My mommy' that, all so dear and adoring."

Lorraine's expression grew cold. "Don't make too much of what Dawn says, Mrs. Baylor," she said scornfully. "She's only three, after all. What can she know?"

"She's a very bright and loving little girl," Mother responded firmly.

"Oof!" Lorraine grunted dismissively with a shrug of her shoulders and walked away.

But she had only gone a few feet when she returned and thrust her face, ugly with anger now, close to Mother's. "You stay away from her from now on, you hear!"

Meridian Day. The day after January the 25th was January the 25th again because we crossed the International Date Line and had to set our clocks back, so to speak, a full twenty-four hours. Dad drew a map of the area we were in to show us the imaginary line that runs north to south along the 180th meridian of longitude from Greenwich. Had we been going in the other direction, he said in explaining the time zones, we would have lost, not gained, a whole day. We passed Sunday Island.

Our ship continued to roll in a treacherous fashion. It was unsettling and tiresome. The floor beneath our feet was never flat, and we kept lurching into walls. During mealtimes we had to keep one hand on our plates to prevent them from scooting away. The tables in the mess were bolted to the floor, but the chairs weren't, and once in a while we all of us would laugh a bit, trying to keep a good face on it, when our chairs slid away from the tables, leaving us with forksful of food held over our vulnerable laps. At night we were frequently awakened by a deep, long roll to one side or the other. We found it difficult to sleep, having to brace ourselves against a steep angle.

The rolling was not quite so sharply pronounced in the hold, Dad and Kevin reported, but it was disconcerting, nonetheless, they said, and it was making the wounded men restless and irritable.

Kevin said, "The fact that they're there is part of the problem. This ship's got no ballast. A hold full of people isn't heavy enough. We should have tons and tons of goods down there to help keep us steady."

Changing the subject somewhat, Mother wanted to know how Mrs. Dobson was faring in the hold and what she was doing to be of assistance to Dad and the other doctors.

Before Dad could answer, Kevin said, "She's wonderful! Prettier than any of the nurses. The men like it that she talks to them. Sometimes I see her talking to one guy, and all the others near him are practically hanging out of their hammocks, listening in."

Mother gave Dad a quizzical look. "Good at giving back rubs and so on, eh?"

"A good deal more than that," he said flatly. "She's been a fine help to us."

"Other than holding their hands and giving them bedbaths, how so?" Mother asked, sounding a bit miffed.

Dad put on his serious, I'm-telling-you-this-as-a-doctor face. "She's expert at changing dressings, and knows about burn treatment. She's quick to spot a developing infection, a fresh fever. And yesterday, for instance, she detected the first hint of gangrene in a man's leg. She's also quick to spot an acute abdomen. And yes, as a result of her talking with the men, she has a good sense for the difference between ordinary grumpiness and an incipient depression."

Mother raised her eyebrows. "What do the military nurses think of this civilian paragon of virtue? And why didn't she say she's an R.N.?"

"To tell you the truth, I think she's more than just a nurse."

Mother's eyes flashed with anger. "Nothing you've mentioned, Sam, is beyond what a good nurse could do or would be alert to! Anyway, what are you suggesting — that she's a doctor?"

"I get the feeling she may well be, and for some reason or other isn't admitting it. I believe she was educated in Europe. She told me she was born in Brussels and married an American there before going to India with him later. It's clear she's had a great deal of experience somewhere."

I said, "She's worked in *ashrams*."

He nodded. "She told me that, too. But I think she has also had extensive medical training. As for her working with the nurses," he went on, acknowledging Mother's earlier question, "she takes orders, just as I do, and they like her. I know it doesn't sound like it, but actually she keeps a very low profile and passes along her observations only to me. Then I check it out and pass it along to one of the medical officers. As civilian volunteers, both she and I are anxious not to step on any military toes. We just do as we're told, help where we can."

"Why don't you ask her about her background?" Mother said sharply.

Dad gave a little not-just-now wave of a forefinger. "I would like her to volunteer the information. Perhaps she will when she feels she can take me into her confidence. Until then, I'm reluctant to pry."

We had a respite from the rolling one day soon thereafter, when our ship dropped anchor near an island. We were not told why we had stopped there, but everyone, including the walking wounded, went up on deck to enjoy the sunshine. The beautiful little island looked like a long green finger with the knuckle bent, for almost in the exact middle of it was a volcanic mountain, its steep sides dropping down into a forest of tall coconut palms, in front of which ran a strip of white beach along the greenish-blue waters of a lagoon. A protective ring of coral islets set this Pacific jewel apart from the dark waters of the ocean. Were one to draw it, people would probably say it was too perfect.

Nevertheless, every true and would-be artist on board, including Kevin, hurried to bring art materials on deck and get to work at depicting this lovely view. For the next couple of hours all of them were busy, bending over sketchbooks, dipping into watercolors, or, as in the case of one man and one woman, standing at large canvases set up on easels, their palettes peppered with glistening blobs of oil paints.

Hugh, Lee, and I stood at the railing, and for a few minutes Mike Turner joined us. The island was called Bora Bora, he said. It was one of The Society Islands, with Tahiti, the best-known of them, lying about a hundred miles off to the southeast.

"Why're we here?" Hugh wanted to know.

"Beats me," Mike said. "We peons don't get told stuff like that. Shucks, lots of times even the cap'n don't know all the reasons he's told to do things. He just goes ahead and does 'em and figures he'll find out why later. All I've heard is a launch will be coming out with crates of coconuts, but you can bet yer bootstraps we didn't stop just for that. My guess is there's a few Navy folks we've gotta take on board and maybe a message or two for the captain, 'cause our blackout conditions pretty much include the airwaves. Incognito and incommunicado are the words for this here trip. That plus zigzagging."

"How do we know there's not a Jap sub out there right now, coming for us while we're anchored?" Hugh wanted to know.

"'Cause one of ours is out there prowling like a coyote that's just littered upwind of a puma," Mike replied.

I was looking at the dark-green water in which we lay, and now I said, full of longing, "If we're not going to get closer to that beach, couldn't we jump off and swim right here?"

"Nah, you wouldn't want to do that," Mike said. "Out here, outside the reef, there's sharks. You keep your eyes open, you might see 'em. Looks like a honey of a beach, though, don't it? And water to knock your eyes out. Peaceful, after all the pounding we've been taking."

"No one's allowed on shore this time, huh?" Hugh asked.

"Nope." Mike pointed. "Look, here she comes! I've gotta get down there and help with those crates."

We three kids stayed at the railing to watch an impressive-looking launch make its way across the spacious harbor, advance through an opening in the reef, and approach our ship. A ladder was flung down, and six Navy men in tropical whites climbed up it, the first of whom was an officer, the three golden stripes on his shoulder boards glinting in the sun. He and Captain Jackson went up to the bridge together.

"Bringing messages," Lee spoke up. "I wonder what about?"

"You needn't look so worried," Hugh said to her. "You think he's come to get you for pretending to be a boy?"

He'd said it jokingly, but Lee didn't smile. She really did look worried, and suddenly I felt sorry for her, sorry that she had things she couldn't mention until the war was over, as she'd said to us that afternoon in Melbourne. What would it be like, I wondered, not to have brothers to talk to? And how would it feel to be traveling without parents? Who are her parents? I wondered again. And why aren't they with her? I wished I could meet her mother. Was it from her Lee had learned how to play chess and mah-jongg and make macramé hangings? If so, she must be a clever lady. And since Lee was so beautiful, was her mother beautiful, too?

But I was beginning to learn not to blurt out every question I had in my head. Dad had said, for instance, that he was willing to wait for answers from Mrs. Dobson until she had gained confidence in him, and that made sense, because if you don't have a person's confidence, you're just going to get half-truths, anyway, and what's the point of that?

But it was an awful strain. Not knowing the answers

to the questions I had was like not being able to scratch mosquito bites: The more they itched, the more I thought of them.

Hugh was talking, and out of my reverie I caught his last words: ". . . going to be a ship's captain, so I'll know what's going on."

"Mike said even the captain doesn't always know," I reminded him. "Anyway, you said you want to be a hepiologist."

"Herpetologist," he corrected me. "Nah, being a captain would be much more interesting."

"But then I couldn't be with you," I pointed out. "You said we'd go back to India together."

"Heck, Jannie, that was baby talk. Someday you and I will be going our separate ways, you know."

"You think?"

"Of course. It's not natural for brothers and sisters to stick that close together."

"But you'll still love me, won't you?"

"Heck, yeah, that goes without saying!" Hugh said.

Our ship's engines rumbled once more, and within minutes a sailor came along to gather up the various works of art.

"Why?" I heard a woman shriek — the one who had been working in oils. She stood staunchly in front of her easel, her arms protectively outstretched.

"Just in case you decide to toss it overboard, Madam."

"But I *wouldn't!*"

"We'd prefer to keep it safe for you. For security reasons, Ma'am."

"Prop it up somewhere then, please," she urged, stepping aside. "Don't lay anything on top of it! It'll take three or four days for it to dry properly. Please!"

"Okay, okay, lady," he said, gingerly picking up the sturdy canvas by its edges. He held it at arm's length to study it a moment. "Hm, can't say this one would be much of a threat to us," he remarked, shaking his head in puzzlement. "It sure don't look like what *I've* been gazin' at all afternoon."

# *Ten*

We had been at sea again for a few days after the brief stop at Bora Bora and had once more crossed the Equator. Only a final wide stretch of the Pacific remained to be navigated.

The family was gathered in our cabin after supper one night. Kevin and Lee were with us, too. We were playing Charades, our own version, in which one didn't communicate syllables and words but acted out for one's own team the essence of a story or song or nursery rhyme that the opposing team had suggested. Dad, Hugh, and Lee were on one team, Mother, Kevin, and I on the other.

The continual pitching and rolling of the ship added to the hilarity of the game when, for instance, Hugh was trying to be Little Miss Muffet who sat on a tuffet, and lost his balance, ending up on the floor under the sink. Or when Mother, in a valiant attempt to depict Robin Hood, reached for an imaginary arrow in the quiver on her back and in a steep roll found herself clutching the linens on Dad's upper bunk.

And then suddenly nothing was funny anymore.

The roll of the ship to its starboard side deepened. And deepened. Much more than usual. The pitch of the floor was now at a steep angle, and Lee, who had stood up to face her team and begin her enactment of "Row, row, row your boat," fell backward onto Kevin's lap. Dad and Mother's survival kits scooted out from under her bunk, followed by the steamer trunk, which slid across the floor, and those of us sitting on my bunk lifted our legs just in time for it to slam against the second steamer under there. From all around us, in cabins nearby and on the decks overhead, came the sounds of crashing and cries of alarm. The ship itself was groaning like a giant, dying.

Kevin looked at his watch.

The light dimmed. The Standby alarm went on. Hugh giggled nervously, and abruptly the alarm was turned off.

The ship was not righting itself!

"Nellie," Dad said firmly, "come here by me."

He reached a hand out to her and pulled her to him as though she were climbing the last few feet of a mountain peak. He settled her next to him and put an arm around her, the other around Hugh. Kevin and I huddled together on my bunk, with Lee still on his lap, her arms wrapped around his neck.

Now I became conscious of the fact that Dawn and baby John were screaming in their cabin.

"Mother, baby John . . ."

"Yes, I hear them. I think they're alone again. I'm wondering . . ."

"We'll go to them as soon as we level out," Dad said.

Kevin said, "It's been four minutes now, Dad. Do you think it's going to come back again? Do you think we'll be okay?"

"Yes, of course. We must trust in the Lord."

" 'Our Father, Who art in heaven . . .' " Mother began the Lord's Prayer, and we all prayed aloud with her in varying tones of certitude:

> " '. . . hallowed be Thy name.
> Thy kingdom come, Thy will be done
> on earth as it is in heaven . . .' "

I was surprised to hear that Lee knew the prayer as well as we did, saying the words in a shaky voice muffled against Kevin's collar.

When we had concluded the prayer, we sat in silence for what seemed to me a long time. (Kevin said later it was an additional minute and a half.)

Then, gradually, with creakings of straining metal, the ship began to right itself. We looked at one another, our eyes wide with hope, our mouths open a little, as though we scarcely dared breathe.

When at last the floor was level again, we all sighed with relief.

Hugh was the first to speak. This time, instead of his imitation of Donald Duck, he did a pretty good job of sounding like Bugs Bunny: " 'What a revoltin' development that was!' " which brought flickers of smiles to Mother and Dad's faces. I noticed then that Hugh's face was whiter than anyone else's.

Kevin said uncertainly, "I wonder if Lee and I should try to get to our cabin now."

The ship began a roll to portside.

"Both of you, stay right here!" Dad commanded.

This roll was worse — faster and more precipitous. The two steamer trunks hurtled across the floor between the bunks, slamming into the opposite wall. Mother, Dad, and Hugh were thrust back, while Kevin, Lee, and I braced ourselves to keep from falling off my bunk. All around us were the sounds of things breaking, and overhead were mighty thumps of big things shifting and rocketing against walls. There were shouts, cries, and screams of terror, among which were the clear sounds of baby John wailing and the shrieks of Dawn in terrible distress.

"Sam, we can't leave them all by themselves!" Mother exclaimed, she herself sounding greatly distressed.

"All right, but you stay here," Dad said. "Kevin, come with me!"

The ship seemed to have settled itself at a steady steep pitch, not dipping lower but not recovering, either. Dad had to scramble up a sharply inclined floor to reach the door.

"Bring diapers!" Mother called after them. "And a bottle!"

When they had left, Hugh said, his voice full of tenderness for her, "Mother, we've had a good life, haven't we?"

"Yes, dear, we have. And we must trust it's not over quite yet."

"But if it is . . . ?"

"Then it is, dear."

"Do you look forward to going to heaven?"

"I think it must be a fine place," she replied gently, "because Jesus said so. But first, I would like, very much, to live long enough to see the three of you get through college."

Dad and Kevin returned, Dad holding the screaming baby and Kevin carrying a pale and sweaty Dawn on his hip. She climbed immediately onto my lap, and Mother did her best to pacify baby John.

Suddenly the ship shifted another degree more sharply over, and we, all of us except for the baby, breathed "Ohh!"

There were a few more heavy thumps above us, followed by an ominous silence, except for the groaning of the ship itself.

After a while Kevin said morosely, "It's been eight minutes now on this side. I think this is it."

Lee climbed back onto his lap.

"Yes, you may be right," Dad replied, his voice heavy with solemnity. "For the ship, perhaps," he added, "but I can't believe this is it for *me*. I can't believe God gave me so many gifts and has blessed all my training and efforts thus far, simply to have it end in such a ridiculous fashion."

His remarks reminded me of Hugh's confidence that he was born for greater things than merely to end up as "shark food," and I looked across the room at him, and saw that he and Kevin were exchanging glances.

"Well, at least He let *you* get quite a long way, Dad," Hugh said bitterly.

Dad looked at him sharply. "I didn't mean just me, of course. I'm confident God has things in store for all of us."

"Hmm," Kevin grunted, "in that case we'd better get ready for the Abandon Ship alarm."

Now Mother and I looked into each other's eyes. How, I wondered, could we be expected to get up to our lifeboat, with the ship tipped over at this angle? Negotiating the ladders would be almost like swinging across monkey bars.

Hugh lifted his chin in his characteristic expression of speculation. "I don't think they're going to sound that alarm," he said, " 'cuz everyone scrambling around might be just the last straw to tip us completely over."

"Possibly," Dad said, "but if it does go off . . ." He reached under Mother's bunk for the four survival kits that were now there. "Kevin, you and Lee must go to our lifeboat with us."

"The little ones, too," Mother said.

"I want my mommy!" Dawn screamed.

Lee suddenly squirmed off Kevin's lap, her face contorted with panic. "Mama!" she cried, toppling toward the door, "I want my mama!"

"Lee!" Kevin shouted, leaping up to catch her around the waist. "You can't go out! You can't go out there alone!"

"Let me go! Let me go! If we're gonna die, I wanna be with my *mother!*"

Hugh and I looked at each other in amazement. Was Lee's mother on board?

"Mommy!" Dawn screeched, pulling against my hold on her.

Kevin had picked Lee up. "Okay, Lee, okay, Lee," he said soothingly, "we'll find her. But for now I'll look after you. You'll be all right. She'll be all right. We're *all* going to be all right!"

He carried her back to my bunk and held her once more on his lap, rocking her a bit as she whimpered against his shoulder.

How nice he is! I thought with a surge of love for my elder brother. How good of him to have taken her at her word, which had seemed to me quite insane. How kind not to belittle her panicky desire to be with a mother

169

who was unknown to us. And how smart not to try to question her just then.

I ran my fingers through the damp tendrils of hair at the back of Dawn's neck and bent to kiss a soft fold at her shoulder. She smelled sweetly sour — so different from the sweaty smell of an adult.

"Your mommy's going to be all right, too!" I whispered.

Now Kevin glanced at his watch and muttered, "Eleven minutes."

I looked at him disbelievingly; I would have guessed it closer to half an hour.

The ship seemed to struggle up a little, but then it lurched back down again.

"Oh God," Dad breathed, looking at the ceiling, "please be with all the men below! Oh dear God, how afraid they must be!"

And then I knew that he, too, was afraid; that for all his trust in God's care and in his own intrinsic value, he had come to realize that this was probably our night of reckoning, and abruptly I pictured Mother standing at the window of my bedroom in Taxila and looking out at the darkening green of the lawn where my brothers and I had played a last game of croquet, and then I saw her pulling the curtains shut. Time to get ready for sleep. Had Lee's mother done that, too? And is she really on board? And, if so, who is she?

I leaned over and whispered to Lee, "Your mother

can be on the lifeboat with us if you tell us who she is!"

"You know her!" she whispered back.

Now Kevin and I exchanged wondering glances.

"Here she comes!" Hugh said, but he was referring to the ship, which was beginning to recover, inch by inch. And, sure enough, this time it didn't fall back, but painstakingly began to right itself.

We sat in absolute silence, waiting for the ship to tip in the other direction again. It did, but in a non-threatening fashion, rolling back up to rights again, rolling the other direction, and back again.

After three or four of these normal rolls, to which we had all grown accustomed, there sounded on the ship, below and above and all around us, a great cheer, and someone had the immediate sense to sound the friendly All Clear signal: HOOOOT! HOOOOT! HOOT!

We remained seated on the two bunks and grinned at one another.

Dad started to sing, his tenor voice sounding off-key, I thought: " 'Praise God from Whom all blessings flow . . .' "

Kevin said wearily, slipping Lee off his lap, "God knows how we feel, Dad, so why don't we just let it rest for once, okay?"

Lorraine appeared at our cabin door, her lipstick spread thinly all around her mouth, her mascara smudged under her eyes. She was barefoot, carrying her high-heeled shoes and stockings in one hand.

"Mommy!" Dawn cried, leaping into her mother's arms and wrapping her legs around her waist.

"Oh, Kitten! Oh, my darling Kitten!" Lorraine exclaimed, hugging her fiercely. "I swear to God, I'll never leave you again! Oh, thank goodness you're safe!" She covered the little girl's face with kisses. "I've been so *worried* about you, my sweet thing! Oh, my sweet, adorable thing!"

"Mommy, I love you so much!" Dawn cried into her mother's neck.

"I know, Kitten! I love you too, baby!"

After kissing her little daughter for a few more passionate moments, Lorraine seemed to become aware of the rest of us in the room. She looked over Dawn's shoulder at my mother and said, her voice suddenly harsh with resentment, "I don't care what you think of me, I *do* love her."

Mother nodded. "Of course you do."

"I suppose I owe you some thanks," Lorraine said sullenly.

Kevin gave her a short laugh with a humorless edge to it and said, "Heck no, lady, not if it hurts so much! But just tell your roommate when she gets back that my mother is still looking after her baby, 'cause I don't s'pose *you'd* be willing to do it!"

"Give him to me!" Lorraine said, stepping across the narrow space and lifting baby John up in the crook of her arm, accidentally hitting his head with the shoes she still held. He broke into fresh screams. She left with the two little ones straddling her hips and slammed our cabin door behind her.

Dad said sternly to Kevin, "Under the circumstances, that wasn't very nice. And furthermore, it's not your place to scold a person who's older than you."

"Ohh!" Kevin sighed, covering his face with his hands. And suddenly his shoulders heaved and muffled sounds of his weeping escaped through his fingers.

"Son!" Dad exclaimed in consternation. "Kevin, what is it?"

After a moment Kevin glanced up at him. "Oh Dad, I'm just so *sick* of trying to be so terribly . . . so . . . *nice* all the time! Because I'm really . . . I'm really *not!*"

Dad quickly knelt on one knee in front of him, bringing his face on a level with Kevin's. "But you *are!* You're a very nice boy!"

"I'm *not nice!*" Kevin said furiously. "And you mustn't keep *expecting* it of me! You expect too much of me. And I'm not a *boy!* I stopped being a boy the minute I got on this ship. If only you knew . . . I have such *thoughts* . . . if only you knew! Half the time . . . half the time I don't even like *myself!*"

Dad gave Mother a bewildered look.

"There, there, Son," he said soothingly, patting Kevin's knee. "I'm sorry I scolded you just now. We've all been under a strain lately."

173

Kevin bit a thumbnail. "Yeah, you especially, I guess. It's okay, don't worry about me."

He rose and held out a hand to Lee. "Come on," he said, his voice sounding very stiff and unfriendly, "let's get back to our cabin and see if your uncle's all right."

Mother jumped up to give him a kiss. "Good night, dear."

"Good night, Mother."

# Eleven

I was just finishing my breakfast — a well-deserved plateful of waffles, swimming in butter and syrup — when Captain Jackson stepped into the room. He looked as though he had very recently bathed and dressed, his sparse hair still plastered wetly back from his high forehead, his uniform showing not a wrinkle. I saw that his paunch had completely disappeared since I'd seen him up close that first day in Bombay. There were pouches of fatigue under his eyes.

Everyone in the room rose to applaud him.

He seemed taken aback by the accolade and hastily gestured for us to resume our seats.

"Thank you for that," he began with a smile. "It was a dreadful night, wasn't it? The Chief Medical Officer reports there were seven broken bones, as well as two heart attacks, neither of which was fatal, fortunately."

He cleared his throat and looked from table to table before continuing. "I've come to give a report concerning what happened last night. But first of all, I want to assure you that I'm quite confident it won't happen again.

"You applauded me just now," he went on, "but, to be quite candid with you, it is the engineers who designed this ship . . ."

He paused and a corner of his mouth lifted as though in ironic amusement. "Italians, they were, and I have to admit it's they who most deserve your praise. I say that because she held on under incredible stress, listing three degrees *beyond which* it was calculated she would not be able to recover. I believe the fact that even our printing press tipped over is without precedent."

Captain Jackson cleared his throat again. "Let me try to explain the circumstances. During the past few weeks we have been navigating in very treacherous waters, both in terms of suspected enemies abroad and the disposition of the seas themselves. To mitigate the danger of the first condition, which is, and remains, a real possibility, I was under instructions to pursue a zigzagging course; and, as a consequence of the second condition, which, daily, is an absolute reality, in combination with the first, last night we came within a hair's breadth of tipping over."

He took a breath and smiled. "I can see by the glazed expressions on some of your faces that I'm not being helpful in explaining this."

A number of his listeners chuckled in a good-natured fashion.

"All right," Captain Jackson said with a grin, "I'll

try again. In the enormous swells of the Pacific, like those we've been experiencing lately, it's more dangerous to steer a zigzagging course for fear of Japanese submarines than it is to steer a straight one and take the risk of being more easily hit. Last night it was the *natural* elements that almost did us in when our ship was caught off balance between a zig and a zag."

"Got it!" Hugh said, and everyone laughed, including the captain.

His face grew serious again. "A contributing factor, I might add, is the fact that we are carrying our wounded men in the hold. And, without adequate ballast, our ship is top-heavy."

I saw Kevin give Hugh a triumphant look, and the captain must have seen it, too, because he said warmly, "You'd already guessed that, had you?"

He turned to the others in the room. "Ladies and gentlemen, I'd like you to know that this young man, Kevin Baylor, has been helping out with the wounded men. Both he and his father, Dr. Baylor, have given generously of their time and talented efforts to be of service."

He began clapping, and everyone joined in.

Kevin looked pleased, and I felt pleased for him. He *was* a nice boy, in spite of his protestations to the contrary.

But now suddenly he was frowning, and to my surprise he stood up. "Captain Jackson, Sir, there's a third person who deserves recognition. She's sitting right there," he said, pointing across the room. "Mrs. Dobson."

"You're right," the captain said. He looked ill at ease.

Mother leaned over and whispered in my ear, "Typical, isn't it? Men just *assume* . . ."

The captain was saying, "Mrs. Dobson, please stand up so everyone can see you."

Mrs. Dobson gave the captain a courteous nod, but she did not smile and she did not stand.

There was some scattered clapping, but if that was the captain's belated attempt to thank her as well, it fell flat.

I saw that Mrs. Dobson was looking across the room at us, and as soon as Captain Jackson had left, she came over to our table. She was wearing a sari again today, a mauve one that looked stunning with her blond hair.

"That was nice of you, Kevin," she said, but I noticed she still wasn't smiling. "I wonder . . . is there some place we could all go where I could talk with you privately?"

"Come to our cabin," Mother suggested.

When we were seated on the two bunks — Mother, Dad, and Hugh facing Mrs. Dobson, Kevin, and me — Mrs. Dobson said immediately:

"I owe you a huge debt of gratitude for looking after my daughter Lily last night."

Our chins instantly tipped up in interest, and I

began to say, "So it *is* . . ." but she quickly raised a hand to silence me.

"Lily and I communicate by means of notes we place in a certain book in the lounge, and this morning I found a note telling me she was with you last night and revealed that I am her mother."

"Well, she didn't *really* . . ." I began.

"I had hoped I could keep it a secret, and to that end I made certain we encountered each other as seldom as possible, but . . ."

I broke in, "So that's why Mr. Huang wouldn't let Lee be with people on C deck except us."

She nodded and went on, "But it was an impossible secret to expect a child to keep, especially in a time of danger such as we experienced last night. So now I believe it would be best if I were to tell you my reasons for keeping our relationship a secret from others. When I have finished my story, you will want to decide whether or not you are willing to help us."

"Is Mr. Huang really her uncle?" I asked.

She touched my hand briefly as if to say, Wait, and soon you'll get your answers.

Looking at my parents who sat directly across from her, she said in a quiet, firm voice, "I am Dr. Anna von Sternberg."

Dad's first momentary response was to nod, since he'd already guessed she was a doctor, but then his eyes widened.

"You're . . . German!"

"I am German, yes."

Hugh and I exchanged worried glances. Dad and Mother didn't like Germans!

"Please explain," our father said stiffly.

Her gaze did not waver. She went on in the same quiet, assured voice, "After earning my medical degree in Heidelberg, and having specialized in gynecology, I came to India to work among the women. I was twenty-seven, and although I had idealistic hopes of working with poor women in village settings, I found myself attracted to the big cities where I could enjoy social contacts with other Europeans." She smiled in a self-deprecating way. "Clearly I was not ready for a life of poverty myself. I could not abandon the comforts and privileges to which I had grown accustomed. I was certainly not yet ready for total immersion in an Indian community."

She fingered the edge of her sari that ran diagonally across her chest, found a loose thread and snapped it off.

"I found work in Delhi. I found friends, and we made the rounds of the tea parties, the cocktail parties, where I met a charming, wealthy Chinese man. Pogogh Chang."

She said the name with intense dislike, and suddenly the tone of her voice became bitter.

"We were married. Lily was born. She was seven when it was brought to my attention that her father

. . . her father was . . . was abusing her . . . abusing her in the . . . in the most unspeakable way."

Looking across at my parents, I saw their expressions alter. They had been listening in stony silence, waiting patiently, it seemed to me, as indeed I was too, for her to get to the part that explained her having taken a false name. But now their eyes narrowed with painful concern and their mouths made O's of sympathy.

"*Beating* her?" I asked in horror.

"No, Janet, he was . . . I don't know how I should . . ."

Kevin broke in, "Jannie, he was pretending to love her in . . . uh, physical ways a father shouldn't do."

I had no idea what he was talking about. But, looking at everyone else's horrified expressions, I was reluctant to ask another question at the moment.

I listened intently as Mrs. Dobson went on to say it was Lily's *ayah* who had alerted her to the situation. The Indian woman was home with Lily after school, when she, the doctor, was still at the hospital. But Mr. Chang had been making a habit of sending the *ayah* away on errands, paying her excessive amounts to, in effect, stay away, and the woman, finally guessing the worst, returned abruptly to the house and confirmed her suspicions.

Understanding now that Lily's father had been doing something bad to her, I blurted out, "Why didn't Lee tell you about it herself?"

Mrs. Dobson shot me an irritated look, but then her expression softened. "I know it would be impossible for you to understand what it means to be afraid of your own father, Janet. But Lily was . . . was terrified of what her father would do to her if she told anyone. She finally confessed to me that he had threatened to . . . to mutilate her."

She'd said the last words with such an awful look on her face, I didn't dare ask her to explain.

After a few moments of silence, she went on, addressing my parents again, "Mr. Huang, who was Pogogh's business partner, assisted me in making plans for our escape from Delhi. There was no time . . ."

"How could you trust *him?*" Mother interrupted.

"Because he's Chinese also, you mean? I trust him because, well . . . I trust him. Implicitly. He is a man of . . . of a different school, I suppose I could say. A man of utmost integrity. One learns, in time, to sense these things."

"I trusted Gabriel, too," Dad said quietly.

"Yes, I read that piece," she said empathetically. "I understand your questioning of my faith in Mr. Huang. But there you are . . . he has not let me down. And you know . . . he was fond of Pogogh, but this thing . . . this thing Pogogh was doing broke all bonds of . . . of fraternity."

She looked down at her hands, and I noticed she had clipped her fingernails and they were no longer polished. They looked like the hands of a doctor.

"Mr. Huang is a much older man," she said. "Perhaps that explains it."

Dad asked abruptly, "Why did you take the name of Ann Dobson? And how was it you happened to choose that very name? I knew of an Ann Dobson years ago."

"Yes, Janet told me. I was shocked when she mentioned it."

She sighed, smoothed an imaginary wrinkle in her sari, and went on, "I needed . . . Lily and I needed to leave India. And Lily needed to go back to school. Clearly, we could not go to Germany. Not anywhere in Europe. I wanted us to go to America. But how were we to do that?

"Mr. Huang had a plan," she continued. "He also would go. He would make arrangements, he said, for Lily to accompany him. So as not to raise eyebrows, Lily would be Lee, his nephew, a boy. But I, in answer to your question, Dr. Baylor, I needed . . . in order to escape from India, I needed a passport in the name of a citizen of one of the Allied countries."

"And so you were able to obtain . . . ?" Dad prompted.

"Yes, with his connections in Delhi, Mr. Huang learned that an American woman by the name of Ann Dobson, a woman born the same year as I, had disappeared. He made himself familiar with her statistics and sent me to a friend of his in the American Embassy where I presented myself as the late Dr. Malcolm Dobson's wife and obtained a passport. Subsequently,

Mr. Huang and Lily completed the necessary documents to allow her to travel with him as his nephew, Lee. It was all quite easily done. But very costly."

"Bribes, I suspect," Dad commented bleakly.

She nodded. "He had to grease a number of palms."

"And Mr. Huang is a man of integrity, you say?"

"Integrity, Dr. Baylor, like truth, has many faces, many gray areas," she responded in a voice that sounded very tired. "Not all of us live in your . . . your black-and-white world."

She leaned forward on the bunk. "Lily and I have been in hiding from her father for the past *three* years. But before we left Delhi, I . . . I did a very foolish thing. I didn't want him to be able to trace me through the bank . . . He had insisted on a joint account . . . so I took four of his most valuable gems as a means of support for us." She shook her head. "It was not only foolish, it was dangerous, because it gave him absolute legal power over me, beyond the power he already possessed — as all husbands in India possess, as ruler of the household. I lived in great fear that he would find us, that he would have me imprisoned or, at the very least, would divorce me and keep Lily to . . . to do as he pleased with her."

Mother's eyes were full of sympathy. "Tell us more about your years in hiding, if you will," she said gently.

Now my European friend relaxed a bit and leaned toward my mother as though toward an ally.

"Lily and I lived in *ashrams,* first in Dehra Dun, then in the Punjab — in Lahore, and later in Saharanpur and

Ambala, where the Hindus keep themselves separate from the Sikhs and are very protective of one another, most especially so in an *ashram,* a community within a community. In each place, Lily and I lived with a Hindu family that was willing to lease one small room to us, and we tried as much as possible to blend in, socially and spiritually. I opened a clinic for women and children, asking them to pay only for their medications, insofar as they were able to do so."

She pressed her palms together in the manner of the Indian greeting and gave Mother a little bow of her head. "It was a difficult time, Mrs. Baylor, but, all in all, it was not a bad experience. The Hindus were good to us. I'm sure they sensed we were some kind of refugees, but they never, not one of them, questioned us or pried into our affairs, and we were never brought to the attention of the local authorities as being in any way suspicious members of their community."

Now she laid her hands, palms up, on her lap. It seemed to me a peaceful gesture, one that invited trust and, at the same time, suggested her vulnerability.

She continued, "It was a time, also, during which I learned a great deal about myself, about priorities in my life.

"And fortunately," she added with a vigorous nod, "I managed to maintain contact with Mr. Huang, my reliable support, my secret lifeline.

"And then one day," she went on, looking more agitated now, "he warned me that, as a German, I must stay in hiding, that Germans all over India were being rounded up in detention camps. I had been living in such seclusion from the outside world, it came as news to me. The news was a great shock to me. Mr. Huang warned me that once Lily and I were taken to such a place, Pogogh would easily be able to find us. There would be no . . . no escape.

"No escape," she repeated in a heavy voice. "That is when Mr. Huang . . . well, I have told you that part."

I said, "So it's *you* who has been Lee's teacher, huh? She said that in Darjeeling . . ."

"Poor lamb, I told her to say that, but she found she didn't know how to make it sound convincing."

Dad rubbed his face as though brushing cobwebs away. "So here you are . . ."

"Here I am, a German, dressed in an Indian sari, pretending to be an American, yes. And it is imperative that, before my true identity is discovered, Lily and I lose ourselves somewhere in the United States. I beg of you to help us to that end."

"Well, sure!" Kevin exclaimed spontaneously.

"Sure!" Hugh and I echoed together.

Dad and Mother gave each other uncertain looks before Dad said, "Under the circumstances, I don't think this is something we can keep entirely to ourselves. Would you not be willing to take Captain Jackson into your confidence, as you have done us?"

"Oh, please . . . please, no, I was depending on . . ."

"It's a convincing story," Dad said sternly. "Why would you object to his hearing it?"

I saw that her color had blanched, but she sat up very straight at this point and said firmly, "Because he's a military man, and in such men there is no room for compromise."

"But in such a man as *I* . . . ?"

She was quick to catch his tone of objection. "I did not mean to suggest that you are a man of compromise, no. But you are a free man, a civilian, who is not required to report to superiors. My having procured a false passport, for instance . . ."

"Well, yes, but I understand your reasons for having done so," Dad said. "I don't condone it, but I understand it." He turned to Mother. "Don't we, Nellie?"

"Oh yes, Sam!" she said, her lovely blue eyes shining in support of his last statement.

Mrs. Dobson (I couldn't help thinking of her as Mrs. Dobson, rather than Dr. von Sternberg) smiled at them as though they were children who did not quite understand. "Well, there you are, you see? The captain might also *understand* it, but his position does not allow him to make a personal judgment about it. He would have to report me. To do otherwise would put him in jeopardy with his superiors, and he will not do that."

"It is the fact of your being German that is the true sticking point here, Dr. von Sternberg."

"Dad!" Kevin exclaimed on a high note of indignation. "There are Germans in America, aren't there? There must be!"

"There are, yes. And many of them are being closely watched, I suspect. I'm sure the war has made things very difficult for those who want simply to go on being American citizens. Your Uncle Ollie wrote . . . You remember his letter, the one in which he told about his German friend who tunes pianos and repairs sewing machines but now is unable to find work. That's how it is these days, Kevin."

"But *we* don't need to be like that!" Hugh put in.

"No, we're *not* like that," Mother agreed firmly.

Dad held up a cautionary finger. "Of course we're not, but the situation we're confronting at the moment isn't quite that simple."

"It is if you let it be," I said.

"It *is*, Dad," Kevin supported me in a pleading tone. "And we've got to think about what it means for Lily, too."

Kevin's remark caused Mrs. Dobson, who had been listening in silence, to make a noise in her throat, a grunt of pain that sounded like "Ya," and my heart stirred in sympathy for her.

"Patras turned out to be a good person, remember, Dad?" I said. "And Mrs. Dobson is a very good person, don't you think? You've *said* so!"

"Yes, she is," he said solemnly, looking across the room at her. "Except for . . . well, I just wish it weren't so complicated."

She stood and adjusted the tail end of her sari over her shoulder. "I think it best that I go now. I leave it to you."

When she had left, we five discussed the situation and found ourselves repeating a number of the questions and answers already posed or suggested. Since we thought her to be a good person, what difference did her nationality make? Her essential nature had not changed on our learning she was Dr. von Sternberg and not Mrs. Dobson. Was the fact that she was German a threat to anyone or, indeed, to our nation? Was every German to be held responsible for the acts of her or his native land?

At one point Hugh threw this question into the room: If we discovered that Lee was Japanese rather than Chinese, would we turn her in?

"You know," he went on, "one time I said to her we'd never allow a Japanese person on this ship, but that was stupid. We've got to take individual cases into account."

"You understand, Hugh," Dad said, "in wartime, individuals don't count for much. Whole nations are perceived as friends or enemies. Did you know that we have . . . that is, the United States has . . . detention camps where Japanese persons are held. Did you know that?"

"No!" we three kids said together in our surprise to hear of it.

Dad nodded solemnly. "I understand many of them are actually American citizens, but their heritage is . . ."

"That stinks!" Hugh exclaimed.

"*War* stinks," Kevin said softly.

"Yes, it does," Dad agreed, "because the innocent suffer along with those who . . ."

"So why does God let it *happen?*" I interrupted heatedly. "We keep praying, 'Thy will be done on earth as it is in heaven,' so if He's so all-powerful, how come . . ."

"Because we're not His puppets, Janet," Mother said quietly. "He gave each of us the right to choose good or evil. It was a wonderful gift, if you think about it. The freedom of choice."

"Except," Kevin inserted sullenly, "some powerful people make evil choices that affect the rest of us. So what's wonderful about that?"

Mother shot Dad a worried, help-me-with-this-one glance, and after a while he said, "Your mother was speaking about *individual* responsibility."

"*Victims* don't get to make choices," Kevin remarked doggedly.

"No, they don't," Dad responded with a sigh. "In the history of the human family there have always been tyrants and victims. There always will be. But I meant that, in the eternal picture of things, all one truly needs to worry about is whether or not one's *personal* decisions are moral or not."

"So, okay, Dad," Kevin said, "we have a personal decision to make right now. Dr. von Sternberg, alias Mrs. Dobson, is a German who holds a false passport. Are we going to report her to Captain Jackson and let *him* make the decision about it?"

"I think we must," Dad replied without hesitation. "Our personal responsibility extends to our behavior as American citizens. I'm sure when the captain hears her entire story . . ."

"But she's a *friend!*" I objected. "That makes a difference!"

"It shouldn't," Dad said firmly. "Even for friends you don't look the other way. If her only offenses are the theft of her husband's gems and the procurement of false passports, I doubt there will be serious consequences, given her desperate circumstances. Her husband has access to her bank account and she has his gems. An equal exchange, perhaps. As for the passports, well, she and Lily may well be regarded as persons seeking asylum, and America looks kindly on such people. But there still is a great deal we don't know about this German woman, and I'm not inclined to take personal responsibility for what is unknown to us."

"So you're going to report her," Kevin said unhappily.

"I'm going to ask to speak with Captain Jackson."

Kevin frowned. "May I go along?"

Dad looked from one to the other of our anxious faces. "You don't trust me to handle this," he said in a resentful tone.

Now we three siblings and Mother exchanged worried glances and then looked down at our laps.

After a few moments, Mother said, "Of course we trust you, Sam."

"We've always trusted you, Dad," Kevin added. "But in this case, you . . . well, frankly, you've got a streak of rectitude down your back as big as a skunk's."

Dad gave him a weak smile. "Not the best of analogies."

Kevin grinned back. "Guess not. Sorry. But as Mrs. Dobson said, you're a black-and-white *moral* person, and the captain's a black-and-white *military* person, and I tend to see things sort of gray."

"Tell you what," Dad responded agreeably, "we'll *all* go to talk with the captain."

But Dad did not make an immediate appointment to see the captain. Nor did he mention the subject for a couple of days.

Kevin, Hugh, and I, however, talked of little else when just the three of us were together. We speculated that Dad was probably talking about it privately with Mother, or maybe he was taking his time to think it over for himself.

My brothers and I worried about what would happen to Mrs. Dobson if her true identity became known to the captain or to the immigration authorities. Would she be arrested? We resolved, in the event that anyone questioned us, we would do our best to support her. But if she *were* arrested, we wondered what would happen to Lee. Hugh thought she should come and live with us while her mother was in jail. Kevin couldn't believe that such a fine person would ever be put in jail.

"You've got a crush on 'er, don't cha?" Hugh said.

"Crush!" Kevin flared. "Oh, come on! Just 'cause I think — "

"He thinks she's a nice lady, that's all," I interceded on Kevin's behalf.

Hugh gave me a scornful look. "You're too young to know what I'm talking about."

"Young!" I flashed back at him. "I hate that word! It's just another way of telling someone she's stupid. Anyway, I think both of you are going overboard worrying about this whole business. I don't want to talk about it anymore."

But we did go on talking about it, particularly on the second day after Mrs. Dobson's conversation with us, when it became apparent that she hadn't yet told Lee about it. We decided not to mention it to Lee unless she herself brought the subject up.

I wondered what Lee must be going through, since she'd spilled the beans the night we'd almost capsized and then she'd written to tell her mother, but now Lee wasn't getting any comfort in being able to talk to us about it.

Sometimes I really questioned the way adults chose to go about things.

# *Twelve*

Our family was playing a word game that same evening when we heard a knock at the door, and Hugh got up to answer.

It was Captain Jackson! He was smiling, but something in his eyes and in the very fact that he was there told me he had a serious purpose in coming. He wore, now that the weather was cooler again, his deep-blue uniform of soft-looking wool, against which the four golden stripes on his sleeves showed up particularly nicely.

"I wonder if I might speak with you for a few minutes?"

"Of course!" Dad said cordially, jumping up to shake his hand. "Do come in. Please sit down." He indicated the spot he had just vacated on the bunk near Mother.

"Then you sit here, Dad," Kevin said, patting the spot between him and me.

"Tight quarters, eh?" the captain remarked.

"Cozy," Hugh said.

Captain Jackson rubbed his chin a few moments. He seemed to be pondering what to say next.

"Dr. Baylor, you've had an opportunity to observe Mrs. Dobson in her work among the wounded men. What is your impression of her?"

If Dad was surprised at the captain's bringing up this subject, he didn't show it. "She's an excellent worker," he replied evenly. "Very competent."

"Competent in doing what, exactly?"

"Competent in each of her duties," Dad replied, rather vaguely, I thought. "She has fine skills. And good intuition. The men appreciate her being there."

I was watching him closely, and now I looked around and saw that Mother and my brothers were, too. I think we were all holding our breath, wondering if and when he was going to tell the captain that our friend was a doctor.

Captain Jackson was looking intently at Dad also. Now he said, "I understand Mrs. Dobson paid a visit to your cabin yesterday morning. Was that for any particular reason?"

Dad's jaw clenched a bit. He did not answer immediately. When his answer came, it was as decidedly cautious as his first answer had been.

"Yes, we'd had our near disaster the night before," he said, as if to imply that had been sufficient reason to have a discussion with any fellow passenger. He added nothing more.

I felt my heart pound with excitement. He's *not* going to tell him! I thought. Not long ago he'd wanted to talk with the captain about Mrs. Dobson, but something's changed his mind since then, and now he's going to keep her secret!

But hang on, I told myself. Maybe he's just waiting to see what the captain's getting at. Maybe the captain has already guessed that she's not really Mrs. Dobson, or maybe he already knows she's not, and he wants to see if Dad and the rest of us know.

If he asks Dad flat out about it, though, I thought, Dad won't tell a lie. He likes her, but he won't tell a lie for her.

"I wonder," Dad was saying now, his voice casually curious, "are you kept informed of *all* of your passengers' movements?"

The captain gave him a tight smile. "No, only a few we need to keep an eye on. And it has come to my attention that Mrs. Dobson is one of them." He pulled at a shirt cuff, concentrating on it as though it were suddenly very important that it extend exactly a quarter of an inch beyond the rim of the coat sleeve.

Neither Dad nor any of us said a word.

The captain looked up, glanced at each of our faces, and went on: "You seem to think well of her, but I must tell you a serious matter concerning her has come to light."

Uh-oh, I thought, here it comes!

The captain rubbed his knees as though they ached

from his recent descent down the ladders or from his present position on the bunk.

He continued: "The U.S. embassy in Delhi reports that certain charges have been registered against her, which prompted the embassy officials to review their records. In doing so, they learned that a person by the name of Ann Dobson arrived in India with her husband, Dr. Malcolm Dobson, in 1933. They noticed, too, that in the intervening years neither of them had had a passport renewed in order to return to the United States. Not in ten years. Highly unusual, wouldn't you say, for a missionary couple to stay on for ten years?"

"In actual fact, it isn't," Dad said firmly. "Our friends, the Fosters, have been in India for the past twenty years. They're going home now to relatives in St. Louis only because of retirement. I doubt very much that the embassy people saw anything particularly unique in that."

"You may be right," the captain said. "I might have been letting my own prejudice show there. It's hard to imagine anyone staying that long in India without a break."

"Part of the reason, of course, has been the war," Dad commented. "It altered the plans of a number of people."

Dad was being polite, yes, but I also sensed he was being resistant, which was unlike him. He was usually respectful of people in positions of authority — and expected the same treatment himself from others. I wouldn't have been surprised if his responses to the captain had been completely cooperative. Until now he has trusted the captain, I thought, remembering the fact that the two men had had a confidential conversation at the beginning of our journey, and just minutes ago Dad had greeted him warmly. But, it seemed to me now, the captain's negative attitude toward Mrs. Dobson and especially his announcement that charges had been brought against her had made Dad very cautious in the way he replied.

" . . . embassy also checked police records," the captain was saying. "The British police keep excellent records, by the way. And, after a considerable search, it was found that Dr. Dobson was murdered, he and the couple's infant son, in Peshawar, in 1935."

I was at that moment looking at my father's hand, spread open-fingered and tense on his thigh, and now I steeled myself not to look up at anyone for fear the captain would see in my eyes that this story was familiar to us.

With an open hand of appeal, Captain Jackson gestured toward Dad. "Doctor, you told me you've been posted for the past seven years in the Northwest Frontier Province. In Taxila, you said. I found it on the map. Not far from Peshawar. I wonder if you heard of the incident?"

"We heard of it, yes. As you must know, it happened a good while before we arrived in the area."

"When you met our current Ann Dobson, however, I imagine the name . . . You recalled the name."

"Oh yes."

"Apparently after the murders, the doctor's wife . . . Well, she didn't leave India, at least not by a conventional route. Do you have any idea what happened to her?"

"People thought she might have been kidnapped by the same Pathan who murdered her husband and child."

I still didn't dare to look up, but I could hear in Dad's voice a clear note of irritation.

"Were you ever shown a photograph of the Dobsons?"

"I was, yes."

"Do you see any resemblance between Mrs. Dobson and the woman you saw in the photograph?"

"Captain, I must tell you I don't appreciate this line of interrogation. Kindly tell us what you're getting at."

"All right, yes . . . yes, I will. Only one American by the name of Ann Dobson entered India, and the one we know by that name is not the same person. We know that now . . . we, that is to say, the embassy people in Delhi know that, by having compared two photographs — an old one of the doctor and his family, which appeared in a publication not long after his death, and Mrs. Dobson's recent passport photo. The two women are clearly not the same person. The most telling evidence is that Malcolm Dobson's wife had a glass eye."

Captain Jackson shifted his position on the bunk across from me. "Do I detect by the glint in your own eyes that you noticed that as well, Doctor?"

"Correct. What exactly do you want from us, Captain?"

I stole a glance at Hugh. His eyes were on the captain, who, it seemed to me, was looking more and more unhappy with this persistent show of resistance from our father.

It was clear to me now that Dad was doing his best to conceal Mrs. Dobson's secret, or, at the very least, was forcing the captain to reveal what he knew about her before admitting what he himself — as well as the rest of us — knew, and I wondered where this line of conversation would lead. I sat absolutely still and kept my eyes on the captain's knees.

" . . . getting to that," he was saying in response to Dad's question. "One name, two women. Another extensive search was embarked on. They had a devil of a time tracking down the true identity of our Mrs. Dobson. They looked at every possible source of photographs of American and European women of Mrs. Malcolm Dobson's approximate age, bearing in mind that certain European embassies had closed in recent years. They finally found an old photo on a hospital work permit. And, to make a long story short, the search revealed that the person we know to be Mrs. Ann Dobson is, in fact, a German by the name of Dr. Anna von Sternberg!"

The captain looked at each of us and said after a few moments of complete silence in the room, "It's obvious this revelation comes as no news to any of you."

"No," Dad said.

"I see. And you did not think it worth mentioning to me?"

"I've thought about it a great deal," Dad replied firmly. "I'm sure each of us has. I came to the independent judgment that she is a woman of integrity, a woman of great worth, who poses no threat to our country, but who, conversely, is in need of asylum in the United States. It seemed to me, having deliberated the matter, that to reveal her identity to you would only serve to jeopardize her chances of realizing the freedom she desires and deserves."

It sounded to me like a speech he'd rehearsed in his head in case he would ever be asked the question, and obviously he'd thought a lot about what Mrs. Dobson had said about the captain being a military person and not free in himself to make such judgments.

The captain pulled on the other sleeve awhile before saying in a sarcastic tone, "Well, Doctor, this woman whom you describe as a person of integrity . . . this woman is also charged with the theft of gems and with kidnapping."

"Kidnapping!" Kevin exclaimed.

"That's right." He shook his head at Kevin and the rest of us like a disapproving teacher in a classroom full of recalcitrant children. "She's charged with kidnapping."

Dad asked heavily, "May I ask who brought that charge against her?"

"Someone by the name of Patel."

"Patel is an Indian name," Dad remarked cautiously.

"Right. He's charged her with kidnapping his daughter."

Hugh and I dared a glance at each other. He mouthed a silent *Shh!* at me.

Dad asked, "Did this Mr. Patel appear in person to make these charges?"

"I have no idea. I imagine so. Why do you ask?"

Dad shrugged his shoulders as though it had been a foolish question, but I knew why he'd asked it: Mr. Pogogh Chang might have given himself an Indian name, but he couldn't give himself an Indian face.

And suddenly I was very worried. Back in Delhi, the embassy people were no doubt going on with their investigation while our ship was still at sea. They would know that Mr. Patel was really Chinese, and by now they would know his original name was Chang. Next they would probably check our passenger list, discover that Mr. Huang, Lee's "uncle," had once been Mr. Chang's business partner, and then they would put two and two together and start looking closely at Lee's passport, too!

I glanced again at Hugh, but he didn't look worried. Instead, his blue eyes were bright with intrigue.

"Captain Jackson," he said, "did you hear this stuff about Mrs. Dobson when we stopped at Bora Bora?"

The captain looked taken aback. "Why do you ask that?"

"It's just that I heard we're running 'incognito and incommunicado,' so I wondered . . ."

"Who told you that?" the captain asked sharply.

"I hear things," Hugh responded guardedly. "And . . . and I've got lots of friends on this ship."

It reminded me of boarding school, when we'd tell each other about how our teachers or our boarding masters and matron would question us about a problem that involved other kids. In school there was one rule we never broke: Don't tell on a friend. And I knew that at this point someone would have to twist Hugh's arm to get him to mention Mike Turner's name if saying it would get Mike in trouble.

"Anyway," Hugh went on, his expression confident now, "you yourself said we'd be under radio silence, so I guessed when that naval officer came on board and went up to your cabin, he was bringing you messages."

Captain Jackson leaned forward, gripping his knees. His hands were pudgy and very pale against the blue of his trousers. He studied Hugh's face a moment and nodded. "Right, I heard about it, among other things, at Bora Bora."

He looked across the cabin at Dad. "If she married

someone by the name of Patel, it will be a matter of record. I'm waiting to hear more when we dock. She didn't come aboard with a child, that's for sure. Maybe she has the girl hidden in a convent and hopes to get her to the States later. But even if the child is her own, I'm told that in India the father would have first rights over the girl."

"Yes," Dad said heavily. "But I might add that it's more likely a girl in India is ignored by her father, rather than sought after. This Patel — a very common name, by the way — is, uh, well, it might be worth investigating his motives in this case."

"Motives?"

Dad sighed. "He's a despicable man, Captain. Mrs. Dobson and . . ."

"Dr. von Sternberg," the captain corrected him.

"Yes. The doctor and her daughter have been in hiding from him for the past three years because he'd been sexually abusing the girl. The charge of theft has to do with the fact that the doctor took four gems from him in order to support herself and the child, having left her own savings in a bank account. It would be interesting to find out what those amounted to, and whether her husband has absconded with them. The point is, I doubt very much if either of his charges would stand up in our courts, given the circumstances. The woman and her child simply fled from him and the unquestioned authority he could exert over them."

Captain Jackson cleared his throat — a sound that

was full of disapproval. It reminded me of a teacher I once had — Mr. Motts — who did that all the time when the class was misbehaving. I found it very irritating.

"She's told you . . . she confided all of this in you," the captain said.

"She did."

"No doubt, then, she also told you where the girl is." He was smiling a bit now.

"She did," Dad said again. "And that's what you really want to know, isn't it? You knew about Mrs. Dobson's true identity, so you didn't need to come down here and tell us about that, but . . ."

"I'd be interested . . ."

"On a personal level? Or were you given instructions to find out?" When the captain didn't answer, Dad went on, "That's what you really came to discover from us. Well, Captain, I'm sorry, but we're not going to help you there."

"You don't trust me," the captain said soberly.

"Not insofar as it might jeopardize the daughter's safe refuge from her father, no, Sir," was Dad's forthright answer. "I wish it were otherwise, but you . . . It's imperative that the girl's whereabouts remain a secret from her father, and it seems to me, ever since you came in, you've tried to prejudice us . . . to make her suspect in our . . ."

"A German woman traveling under a false passport, as far as I'm concerned, *is* suspect, Doctor!"

"I've explained that."

"No, *she's* explained it to you!"

"Well, you see," Dad said quietly, "I believe her."

He rubbed his forehead with all ten fingers, as though he had a headache, but Dad never got headaches.

He looked up at the captain. "Sir," he said earnestly, "once before in my life I judged a person without hearing his side of things, and . . ."

Kevin interrupted, "Dad, I could go get her right now and have her come tell all about it herself. She'd tell the captain herself, don't you think, if we were here?"

"Good idea," Dad said.

"Not such a good idea," the captain said. "My orders are she's to have no hint that we're on to her, not until she's detained by Immigration in San Pedro."

"Oh dear," Mother murmured.

Captain Jackson stood and straightened the jacket of his uniform. "I trust our conversation tonight will remain confidential." He looked at each of us with stern eyes. "Do I have your word on that?"

Mother gave him an apologetic little smile. "I'm afraid we can give you no guarantee about that, Captain. Janet's fond of Mrs. Dobson. All three children are. I have a feeling they'll tell her all about it first thing tomorrow."

The captain was scowling. "Surely, if you ordered . . ."

"Well, you see," Mother said calmly, "that wouldn't be fair, nor very realistic, because they feel a greater loyalty to her than to you."

"That puts me in a spot, then," he said unhappily.

"Yes, I suppose it does," she said. "I'm sorry about that. But if you were to look at it from Mrs. Dobson's point of view, it's not very nice for all of us to be talking about her, and she not knowing about it."

"But it will give her time to prepare a story," the captain said doggedly.

"But she won't, you see," Dad put in, "because *we* know her story. I doubt she'll try to change her stripes between here and San Pedro. And, Captain, I must tell you," he added in a firm, confident voice, "if things go badly once we're in the United States, that is to say, if she finds herself in difficulty regarding these charges her husband has made against her, I will intercede on her behalf, be sure of that."

"I understand. Good night, Doctor." He shook Dad's hand.

"Good night, Captain."

Captain Jackson gave the rest of us a sharp nod, and we murmured "Good night" in a cheerless fashion as he left.

My head was so full of the captain's visit to our cabin that it took me a while to get to sleep that night, and in my mind I kept hearing the things that had been said. I was so proud of my dad and mother for sticking up for

Mrs. Dobson. Not long ago — but it seemed like ages — I wouldn't have bet two pins on their coming to her defense, especially if it meant opposing the captain. I'd loved it when Mother said we kids felt a greater loyalty to Mrs. Dobson than we did to the captain. Mrs. Dobson had been right about him; he had "orders" he had to follow. When the captain himself had said that, I sort of understood it, and I wasn't mad at him, but I felt sorry for him — that he couldn't just follow his heart. Adults, I thought, got themselves into pickles sometimes, having to take orders from bosses they didn't basically agree with, maybe.

So, now what? When we got to California, what would happen to Mrs. Dobson and to Lee? Maybe the Immigration people would put handcuffs on her, and Lee, as Hugh said, would have to come live with us. But of course we'd warn them first, as Mother said. We certainly couldn't let it all come as a surprise to them. Some surprises, like finding my koala, were fun, but some weren't. There'd been a boy in my class, for instance, who liked to play practical jokes. (His name was Alexander Benjamin Carter; we called him ABC.) You'd open your desktop, and there would be a snake crawling around among your books. Or you wouldn't notice the little wire lying across your desk chair, and you'd sit and get a terrific shock because the wire was attached to a battery he'd taped under the seat.

And oh, I thought, hadn't Dad been good when he'd said, "I'm sorry, Captain, but we're not going to help you there," and the captain went away without knowing that Mrs. Dobson is Lee's mother, and that Lee is on board.

In the darkness of our cabin, I heard my dad roll over on his upper bunk, and then Mother, on her lower bunk, punched her pillow and sighed. Then Hugh stirred on his bunk above me, and I could tell by the sound of it he was half-sitting when his voice came quietly, "'Nite, everybody. Dad, Mother, thanks for not squealing on Lee."

"Everything will be all right, Hugh," Dad said soothingly. "When you kids see Mrs. Dobson in the morning, tell her as exactly as you can remember everything that was said here tonight. That will help. Go to sleep now."

# Thirteen

At breakfast, I saw that Mrs. Dobson was sitting by herself, as usual, reading a magazine while she picked at her food. She wore a red sweater and her hair was in one long braid hanging down her back.

"Let's tell 'er," I said when Mother and Dad got up to get themselves more coffee.

"Right," Kevin said. "In case anyone's watching, it will look better if *we*, not Dad and Mother, talk to her."

Hugh nodded. "The last thing Dad said last night was it's okay if we tell her. For some reason or other, he doesn't want to be the one to do it."

"He doesn't want to go against the captain that openly," Kevin said with a grin, "but, as Mother said, they can't help it if we kids do. I'll go make an appointment."

He quickly got up, went over to Mrs. Dobson, bent to say something, and was back in his chair before our parents returned with their full cups. Dad had a second helping of apple strudel.

Later, while Mother and Dad exchanged greetings with the Fosters, Kevin told Hugh and me, "Ten o'clock. Her cabin. C7."

She had the cabin all to herself and had decorated the walls with watercolors.

"Who painted this? You?" Kevin asked in admiring tones as he examined one of them, of a black horse in a field of poppies with snow-covered mountains in the distance.

"Yes," Mrs. Dobson said quietly. "It's a scene I recalled from Kashmir."

"Oh, I love this one!" I said, pointing to another painting that showed a Bengal tiger batting with a paw at a stream that gushed from between moss-covered rocks. The tiger seemed to be having fun.

"That one's not entirely honest," she said. "I left out the bars. I saw that tiger years ago in a zoo in Karachi when our ship docked there for a few days."

Hugh, who was studying a different watercolor, said, "And this is Lee when she was about eight, huh?"

I went to look at it. I hardly recognized Lee. The girl in the painting had Lee's beautiful eyes, yes, but her dark hair hung down to her shoulders and she was dressed in a Punjabi outfit. She was holding out about a dozen garlands at arm's length.

"I copied that one from a photograph," Mrs. Dobson said with a smile. "It was her birthday, and our friends in Lahore put all those garlands around her neck, but she took them off because the marigolds made her sneeze."

She sat abruptly on one of the lower bunks. "You didn't come to look at my artwork, though, did you? Please, have a seat."

When we were seated, Kevin said without beating around the bush, "Captain Jackson came to our cabin last night. He knows who you are."

Mrs. Dobson made no exclamation. She made no immediate comment whatsoever. Instead, she gave Kevin a searching look and then with her left hand took hold of her long braid and began to stroke her cheek with it.

At length she whispered, "He knows I'm German."

"Yes."

She closed her eyes for a few moments. "And what did your father say?"

"Dad was wonderful," Kevin said. "Mother, too. They're both on your side."

She tossed the braid away from her face and sat up very straight, asking fiercely, "Does the captain know about Lily?"

"No," Kevin replied. "Captain Jackson knows you have a daughter, and he tried hard to find out where she is . . ."

"Why? Why did he want to know?"

"Because you've been charged with kidnapping," Kevin told her in a flat voice.

"Kidnapping!"

"Yeah, that's exactly how I reacted."

"That devil!" she exploded. "He wants to have me arrested in California so he can get Lily back!"

We three kids nodded soberly.

Hugh said, "Mr. Chang calls himself Patel now. That's the name he gave when he went to the U.S. embassy to file the charges against you."

"Stealing, too," I put in. "He's charged you with stealing his gems."

Mrs. Dobson put her elbows on her knees and rested her head in her hands. My brothers and I looked at one another in miserable silence.

She lifted her head. She was sniffing a bit and went to the sink to blow her nose. She turned to give us a wan smile. Her face was pale.

"Thanks," she said softly. "Thanks for warning me."

"Dad said we could," I said. "He doesn't want you to be taken by surprise when you meet the Immigration people."

"He told the captain he would come to your defense, if need be," Kevin assured her. "We all will."

Mrs. Dobson sat on the bunk again. "All right, I feel a little better now. Tell me everything the captain said, please. Try to remember exactly what he said and what you and your parents said. And, most particularly, try to remember what you *didn't* say, what you didn't reveal to him."

213

Kevin proceeded to tell her about it as accurately as he could, beginning with the captain's first question to Dad about her work with the wounded men in the hold. From time to time Hugh and I inserted a particular detail that had made an impression on each of us.

When, in the course of his narration, Kevin mentioned the name of Patel again, Hugh interrupted to ask Mrs. Dobson, "Did you know he gave himself an Indian name?"

She nodded. "Mr. Huang wrote me about that. Pogogh added that name to his own in forty-one, right after I left him and went into hiding with Lily. Mr. Huang was still working for him then, and he thought Chang had done it for business purposes. But," she added bitterly, "I knew he'd taken an Indian name to bolster his legal status over us."

Kevin went on to tell her that the captain had surmised she'd left Lily in a convent somewhere in India.

On hearing that, Mrs. Dobson's expression brightened for a moment but immediately clouded again. "By the time we get to San Pedro, they'll have figured everything out, I suspect," she said with a haunted look. "I simply don't know what I'll do."

"Just tell them the truth," Kevin said firmly. "Just like you did to Dad and Mother. You won them over, remember? It took a while, but last night Dad told the captain he believes you. He said that even though you're German, you're a good, worthy person who deserves sanctuary in the United States and that the charge of kidnapping wouldn't hold up in our courts, especially if you told them why you took Lily away."

"He *said* that?" Mrs. Dobson asked, her expression full of a mixture of delight and relief.

"Yes," Hugh said, "and I liked it, too, when he said someone should look into how much you left in your bank account in Delhi, in case it's as much or more than the stolen gems were worth."

"Oh, bless his heart! You know, I might not have thought of pointing that out, but, it's true, I left lots of money there, my whole inheritance, and Pogogh no doubt has it all now."

She buried her face in her hands again, but this time her shoulders were much more relaxed. And when she looked up again, I saw hope in her eyes.

"Oh, I'm so grateful . . ."

"It's no fun," Kevin broke in quietly, as though he'd guessed what she was about to say next. "It's no fun to feel all alone."

"No," she whispered, "it's no fun at all."

"In that case," I said to Mrs. Dobson — because I could see right then that she and Kevin were feeling a bit sorry for themselves — "well, uh, I think you should tell Lee about what's going on, too, so she won't feel so lonely, either."

Mrs. Dobson gave me a sharp look, and then her expression softened. "You're right, Janet. She needs to know, too, about what lies ahead of us. I'll write her all about it tonight."

"I don't know why you need to *write* her about it. Why can't you just *tell* her about it? Everything's going to come out in a few days, anyway, so why don't you just *talk* to her, like you do to me. No one's gonna guess you're her mother, just 'cause you talk to her."

"Ooohh!" Mrs. Dobson breathed and began to stroke a cheek again with her braid. " 'Out of the mouths of babes . . .' "

"I'm not a baby," I said firmly.

"No, you certainly are not. I meant it as a compliment. It's a quote from the Bible."

"I know where it's from."

"Then you know it means that often young people are far wiser than adults are. I'll talk with Lily tomorrow."

The following evening Hugh and I went to Kevin's cabin to invite him and Lee to go with us to watch the "garbage detail." Neither of them had ever seen it. It seemed a silly entertainment to ask people to share, but it was better than staying cooped up in the cabin, and, anyway, our main motive was to find out if Mrs. Dobson had indeed told Lee about the recent complications and about what lay in store for the two of them.

It was very unsteady underfoot on the aft deck, and

the swabbies weren't happy to see us there. They made us stand to one side and instructed us to hold on tightly to the railing.

It wasn't as much fun as it had been the first time. The water was so turbulent we didn't see any fish leap up to grab the garbage, and in the overcast sky there was no moonlight to shine on the silverware, if, in fact, any had been tossed overboard that night.

"What's so interesting about this?" Kevin said grumpily.

"Nothing much," Hugh said. "I just thought the fresh air . . ."

"Not so fresh, though, is it?"

"You're right. Let's go back."

As we were retracing our steps through the maze of dimly lit passageways, Lee said in a small voice, "I'm scared."

We all stopped in our tracks.

" 'Scared.' Why?" I asked. "Your mother told ya, huh?"

"This morning, in the lounge," she said in a tiny voice. "She's in trouble."

"She'll be okay, you wait and see," Kevin said. "You'll both be okay. And if you aren't, you just ask our dad to help out because he can do just about anything. We're your friends, you know."

Lee burst into tears. It was the first and only time I saw her cry. I put my arms around her, while Hugh patted her arm and Kevin patted her head, murmuring, "Oh, girl, don't be afraid."

She quickly got a grip on herself and shrugged us off.

"I haven't been to school in a long time," she said with an embarrassed little laugh. "I won't know anything!"

"You're kidding!" I said. "You know lots of things!"

"I'll bet you even know math," Hugh said. "I'll bet your mother taught you that, too."

Lee nodded. "It's my best subject. She taught me geometry, too."

"Well, there you are!" Kevin said with a comforting chuckle. "To this day I don't know a hypotenuse from a hybrid."

This sent Lee into appreciative giggles. (Later I had to ask Kevin what both of those terms meant.)

"But look, Lee," Kevin went on, his expression serious now, "I suggest when you get to school you don't show off about it, okay? For all I know, you're a ten-year-old whiz of some kind, but other kids don't like whizzes much. Especially not *girl* whizzes."

Lee frowned. "Do I have to pretend I don't know things?"

"Yeah, that would help," Kevin said. "Teachers hate it when kids know stuff already. You could pretend you don't know things but have the knack of catching on real fast. That way you'll get an A and your teacher will like you a lot. That way no one's the loser."

"Okay," Lee said solemnly, "I guess I can do that. It will be like playing a game."

"And you're good at games," Hugh put in.

"Everything's a game," Kevin said. "All you have to know is the rules."

As we drew closer to the mainland ("Only four days away," Mike told us one evening), I was filled with a strange feeling of anticipation and anxiety combined. Soon I would be seeing my "homeland," but home is a place you feel comfortable in, not a place you have to get used to. I wondered if I would like it. But first, before I ever set foot on American soil, there were Mrs. Dobson and Lee to worry about. Would the American officials arrest her or turn both of them away? Or, here's hoping, would they be allowed to get off the ship and be free to live in my country? What *was* my country? What did that mean?

Then, during the afternoon of the following day, February the 5th, we had our final scare at sea.

The swells were not as fearful as they had been, and while Mother and Dad went to the lounge to write letters to be posted from California to relatives in Michigan, my brothers and Lee and I were allowed by the S.P. to go on deck.

It was a bleak, windy day. We buttoned up our jackets and promenaded vigorously for a while. At length, we rested at the railing and stared out at the charcoal waters that spumed cold white spray up into our faces. Not another person that we could see was out and about. In spite of my company, I felt lonely and depressed.

"Just for once," Kevin said wistfully, "I want to go on the forward deck and stand near the guns."

We weren't allowed up there, but Kevin said, "Heck, no one will see us. Looks like everyone's taking a nap."

"Let's go!" we three younger kids said.

"But we can't go straight from here," Kevin said. "How'd you and Janet get there that night, Hugh?"

"I'll show ya!"

We made our way back down to C deck and then followed the route Hugh and I had taken. This time we encountered no S.P.s whatsoever. Maybe after so many weeks at sea they had been relieved of their duties of looking after us civilians.

The four of us stood at the base of the biggest of the weapons, the five-inch 50-caliber gun Mike had told us about. Mounted on a platform, it looked formidable. I wanted to climb into the gunner's seat in the metal tub, but I didn't dare. After admiring the gun and its smaller neighbors for a time, we stood at the railing and once again stared out to sea.

I think we all saw it at the same time — a sharp white line cutting across the dark water at some distance from us, and then, yes, the line was being created by something protruding above the surface, something that looked like the long neck and tiny head of the legendary Loch Ness monster.

"Periscope," Kevin said, and at that moment the shriek of General Quarters sounded: KOO — EEE — YOO! followed by the fierce bells.

Before we could get to the ladder, sailors in gray helmets came rushing on deck, some of them still pulling on their orange life jackets, their faces flushed with urgency. Various commands and expletives rang out.

We flattened ourselves against the wall of the bridge house just as a firm voice on the loudspeaker said: "Submarine off the port beam. Man your battle stations!"

We watched as the 50-caliber gun was swiveled out and the gunner leaped into the metal tub and urgently leaned forward to crank the long gray barrel and take aim. Meanwhile other crewmen were carrying out huge bullet-shaped shells. Other young men were rolling out fire-fighting equipment.

The periscope disappeared, and suddenly everything was quiet, except for the wind.

What were they thinking, all these men in uniform, standing so tensely and expectantly? Were they waiting for orders?

Kevin whispered, "I don't see what good that gun would be against a submarine. We need depth charges."

Oh. I steeled myself for the big bang, the great shudder of the ship under us, and the alarm to abandon ship.

Kevin must have been thinking the same thing because he said, "I think Lee and I will get in your boat."

"Mother and Dad must be having kittens," Hugh said in a small, miserable voice.

We kept our eyes on the heaving gray water and, as we watched, a bubbling and turbulence began to whiten the surface. The submarine began to show itself, first the part that Kevin said was the conning tower and then, with a mighty WHOOSH! the entire sleek, water-shedding length of the submarine rose up. It was scary.

A few seconds later, HOOOOT! HOOOT! sounded our All-Clear signal just as the lid of the conning tower opened and a man appeared, and HOOOT! HOOOT! the submarine answered back. The man held up an American flag and the sailors on deck cheered.

We four ran to the railing and waved to the man. He waved back.

I felt an enormous sense of relief. Just moments ago I'd thought of the sub as a monster, a beast that carried a torpedo to destroy us, but now it seemed the embodiment of a trim guard dog that would look after us until we were safely home.

Kevin and Lee went in search of Mr. Huang. Hugh and I went down to find Mother and Dad, and met them on a ladder, coming up.

"It's one of ours!" Hugh told them excitedly. "Come up and see it! It's beautiful!"

It was still above water, running alongside us, a number of men standing now on its decks.

Mother waved to them, and the men whistled. She blushed with pleasure. "It's not exactly beautiful," she said, "but it's comforting. Do you suppose they're here to escort us?"

"I don't imagine they'll stay right beside us, no," Dad said, "but I think from here on in we're safe from the Japanese."

"Good," she said. "Then we have only one more thing to worry about."

# Fourteen

"We're in sight of land," our mess steward told us at breakfast one morning three days later, and the five of us hurried up on deck.

Other passengers were already there, exclaiming over the fact that we were arriving at last and pointing to the strip of land on the horizon.

"America!" Mother said with a sigh of relief.

"Yes, home again, Nell," Dad said, holding her hand.

Hugh waved as though there were people out there who could see us. "Hello, America!" he shouted.

Kevin said, "I can't wait to go down the gangplank and really be there!"

I looked from one thrilled face to another. In all of the years I could remember, my family members had spoken of our homeland in terms that were invariably positive, except for the fact that its President was a Democrat, the implications of which were lost on me. By the end of 1941, however, even the negative comments about Franklin D. Roosevelt had worn thin and then had stopped altogether. It was right, my parents said, that he'd supported our Allies, especially the British, and of course we had to enter the war when our own territory had been violated by the Japanese. I sensed that respect for the President and love of our country were second only to reverence for God and belief in the teachings of the Bible; and my parents' great enthusiasm, as well as their confident trust in all of these matters, was catching.

But now, seeing the long land mass ahead of us, which seemed to be drawing no closer, I wondered what to expect. I was excited about the promised adventure of discovering a new country, but suddenly I missed India again, the land I grew up in and knew and loved.

I asked hesitantly, "What's so special about America?"

"It's a free country, Jannie!" Kevin said impatiently, as though that were a consideration too obvious to bother mentioning, except to someone who was truly stupid.

"It's the greatest and most powerful nation on earth," Dad said with a clear note of pride in his voice.

"Its streets are clean and there are no beggars," Mother added.

Her remark was the only one that made sense to me. But I *liked* India's streets: The beggars and the litter, I thought, were only a part of being among the interesting people and in the midst of the sounds and colors and smells, such as I'd last experienced in Bombay.

"We'll eat steak and hot dogs," Hugh put in. "And ice cream. And we'll never have to drink buffalo's milk again!"

But I *liked* India's foods. I hadn't had curry in six weeks, and I missed it. I could live the rest of my life without steak and hot dogs, I thought rebelliously, but not without curry and India's tasty breads and sweets. I had to admit, however, that the American milk we'd had on board ship was wonderful, and I wouldn't mind not having to drink water-buffalo's milk ever again. Although our cook had boiled it, to make it safe to drink, it still had tasted a bit muddy, as I imagined the underbelly of the animal to be.

"You'll like America, you'll see," Dad said with a happy ring to his voice.

"You'll see!" Kevin echoed.

"It's time you were back in school, Janet," Mother said, apropos of nothing, I thought, but Dad quickly added, "Yes, it's time you learned more about America, some American history. Time you became a real American."

A *real* American, I thought; what did that mean? I had always been made keenly aware of the fact that I was an American. In boarding school at Ridge Point, for instance, we Americans had unquestionably re- garded ourselves as the dominant force among the students who represented as many as forty-three different nationalities. In student government, sports, dress codes, and speech patterns, we were the controlling factor. A new American would arrive, for example, and within days everyone would be using the latest slang and envying (and trying to copy) the current U.S. styles, whereas no one paid any attention to a new arrival from anywhere else.

But soon I would be going to an all-American school, I mused, and that would be quite different from being in an international school, wouldn't it? Furthermore, I knew my brothers and I would be going to private middle and upper schools — Christian schools, in fact, run by a denomination that was similar to ours, so obviously there wouldn't be Catholics or Jews, Hindus or Moslems, Sikhs or Buddhists there.

Wanting to register my hesitation about this new school I'd have to enter in the middle of the second semester, I muttered unhappily, "So everyone will look exactly like me."

"No one looks like you!" Hugh said with a little laugh.

"You either!" I snapped at him. "*No* one's gonna be as skinny as you!"

I turned to Dad. "But everyone with white faces and all of 'em Christian, huh?"

"Well, yes, I imagine so," he said, giving me an impatient look.

"Sounds boring," I stated flatly. "Why do I have to go to that kind of school? America isn't *all* white and Christian, I know that much!"

"You're right, it's called the great melting pot, but . . ."

"But the private schools are segregated," Kevin broke in, and I heard in his tone of voice that this was something he wasn't particularly looking forward to either. "The private schools keep the meat and potatoes apart."

"And we all know Jannie's a potato!" Hugh said in his Donald Duck voice so I wouldn't be offended.

I was, though; I was feeling edgy and turned on him to ask if he would like to go to a school just for the ones that were chicken bones.

"Better bones than blub!"

"You don't have to get so prickly!"

"Me! 'Prickly!' That's like a porcupine criticizing a hedgehog!"

"At least you admit you're the measly hedgehog," I said loftily, proud of myself for having gained the upper hand.

"That's enough of that!" Mother reprimanded us both. She patted my hand that was gripping the railing. "You'll like the school, Janet. I should think you'd like any school, you're such a good student and . . ."

"And *we* aren't," Kevin interrupted sullenly, referring to himself and Hugh.

Oh dear. Another touchy subject, because neither of

my brothers had liked boarding school or their teachers, whereas I had, so that C and D were common grades on their report cards, and I rarely had a grade lower than an A — a sore point with Dad, who wanted his sons to become doctors, like him. (It was never mentioned that *I* could also be a doctor someday; girls were nurses, like Mother.)

"Of course you are, Kevin," Dad said sharply. "Both of you are fine, intelligent boys. You just haven't . . . haven't found yourselves yet."

"What on earth is the matter with all of you this morning!" Mother exclaimed. "Here we are, almost there . . . I thought we were happy just a minute ago!"

Dad rubbed his arms. "For one thing, it's cold up here. Makes me feel a bit snappish, too." He gave each of us kids a sympathetic smile. "Now that we *are* almost there, I think we're all beginning to wonder about what lies ahead. There's that old fear of the unknown."

'Fear of the unknown' stuck in my head. So he's worried about it, too, I thought. Sure, because he has to get a job right away to pay for a house and a car and winter coats and boots. And if he works in a hospital, he won't be the boss of it, and that will be a big change for him.

Kevin said, "It's not what's coming up later but what's gonna happen to Mrs. Dobson and Lee today that's worrying me."

"Yes," Dad said, "that too. But it'll be a while before we're there, so what do you say we go back down to the mess and see if they'll give us some nice hot chocolate, eh?"

In a far corner of the mess sat a man, smoking a cigar. He looked familiar. It was Mr. McCullough! I hardly recognized him, he was so pale. He was wearing a suit and looked disappointingly ordinary.

"I wanna go talk to him," I said to Mother.

"Who?"

"That man there. Mr. McCullough."

"Why would you . . . ?"

"I just wanna say hello. You comin' with me, Hugh?"

We went up to him. "Hi, Mr. McCullough. Remember us?"

He seemed puzzled for a moment, but then his hazel eyes brightened. "Why yes, you're the Baylor kids."

Hugh said, "We're sorry Mr. Caldwell died."

"So am I." He turned his head away and puffed on his cigar. He blew the smoke away in a great cloud and, waving it away from his face, regarded us for several moments before he said, "I think he knew it was coming. I think he was at peace with it. Well, at least I know he certainly was very tired of being so sick."

Hugh nodded sagely. "Dad says when a person's liver gets that bad, there's nothing much to be done about it."

Mr. McCullough said curtly, "You kids can sit down, provided we can change the subject."

Hugh and I pulled up chairs. We sat. No one spoke.

Growing uneasy with the silence, I said, "They let you out, huh?" It was a stupid question; of course they'd let him out. I quickly added, "Was the brig awful?"

"Awful," he said. "This is my first smoke in a month."

I shook my head at him. "You shouldn't take it up again."

He shrugged. "Everyone's allowed at least one little vice."

"Mine's chocolate," I agreed. "Chocolate and all the other fattening stuff."

Now he smiled — such a nice smile with twinkling eyes.

I smiled back. "You're all dressed up in a suit. Does that mean you're done with snakes?"

He didn't answer immediately. He was looking around for an ashtray, but there weren't any in the mess because people weren't allowed to smoke in there. With a grunt of exasperation he smashed his cigar out in what was left of some cherry pie on his plate.

Hugh was obviously interested to know the answer to my question, and asked, "So, Mr. McCullough, are you going to go on being a herpetologist?"

The man shook his head. "I don't think so. I've done that. It's time to move on to something else."

"Like being a ship's captain? Something like that?"

Mr. McCullough laughed. "Heavens no! Do you

have any idea what a lonely life that must be? No, I need people. That was one good thing being in the brig taught me."

He scratched his head as though it helped him to think more clearly. "I think I'd like to be a science teacher. I think I might enjoy that."

Hugh said, with happy eyes, "That's exactly what *I* want to be. Yeah, I think it would be great if you did that. And, holy catfish, won't you have interesting stories to tell!"

I saw that my parents and Kevin had finished their cups of hot chocolate and were preparing to leave. Hugh and I hadn't had any yet, I thought with regret, but then I felt suddenly proud of myself for choosing to talk with Mr. McCullough rather than indulging in all those calories I didn't need. (The fact that Hugh needed them was, after all, not my concern.)

Shaking his hand, we said goodbye to Mr. McCullough and wished him luck in his new job.

Our family went up on deck again. From a distance, as we drew closer to the port, everything looked clean and shiny — a bustling, modern wonderland. Hundreds of cars were zooming along. I'd never seen so many, going so fast! Beyond the port, the windows of the tall buildings of Los Angeles sparkled in the midday sun.

Mike Turner found us on deck. "Watch out for those snowstorms in Michigan," he said with a grin. "Bundle up!"

Mother told him we were staying in California for a week and then would be taking the train, a three-day trip.

"That'll be fun," he said, ruffling Hugh's hair. "You'll get to sleep in those Pullman compartments. That's a treat."

He pointed to an approaching launch. "Here comes the pilot to take us in. The guys in the black hats are Customs and Immigration. Say, I hear they're lettin' the passengers off first, 'fore they start unloading the wounded."

"And you?" Mother asked. "When will you be able to get away?"

"Not 'til the unloading's over. A couple of weeks from now I get leave, just in time for the azaleas! And in my mom's front yard there's a big ol' magnolia that'll be poppin' soon with blooms." He shifted uncomfortably. "Golly, I do hate goodbyes, so I'll just make it quick."

He shook Dad's hand. "It's been a mighty pleasure to know you, Sir. You've got a grand family here. You too, Ma'am," he said, giving Mother a little bow.

"Your mother will like the perfume, Mike. I certainly do. Thanks again. Thanks for everything you've done to make this trip easier. The children . . ."

"Heck, they've been like family!" he exclaimed, patting each of us affectionately. "Y'all take care, hear?"

He touched his cap, did a smart about-face and was gone.

As the ship approached the dock, we saw the long lines of military trucks and ambulances. Mother and Dad were expecting Dutch friends, the Van Andels, to meet us, but we soon noticed that no ordinary civilians were on the dock, only men and women in uniform: Navy and Army and Red Cross personnel, port officials, and the men of the Shore Patrol.

"As soon as we clear Customs, I'll give the Van Andels a call," Dad said. "It's just as well they're not here because the whole business could take hours."

"I hope not," Mother said. "I'm getting a headache."

"Not now!" Dad said.

"I didn't *ask* for it, Sam," she replied, sounding hurt.

"No. Well, let's hope we can find a place where you can rest, Nellie, because I'm afraid this will be a long process. The men who came for the steamers said even our crates would be inspected."

"What! You've nailed them shut!"

"They have tools."

"Oh dear, and I packed everything so carefully!"

Dad's jaw clenched, but he patted her arm reassuringly as he said, "They'll put things back the way they found them, Nell."

"But what about Mrs. Dobson?" Kevin asked anxiously.

"And what about Lee?" Hugh and I asked almost in unison.

Dad replied calmly, "If the doctor finds she has need

of us, she'll ask to have our assistance. Until such time, I think it would be unwise to assert ourselves."

"But . . ." Kevin began again with a frown.

"I promise you," Dad addressed us three kids solemnly, "we won't leave the dock without determining their status with Immigration."

Holding my koala with one hand, my other hand tightly clasped in Hugh's, I walked down the gangplank with him.

"We're here, Jannie!" he said happily, flashing his crooked teeth at me.

But *here* was just the dock, where we stood in line for the next hour, waiting our turn to be cleared by Customs. I kept looking for Mrs. Dobson and Lee, but I didn't see them. Nor was Mr. Huang standing in any of the lines.

Then I saw Dao-Zeun!

I ran up to him. "Hi, Dao-Zeun. Where's Mr. Huang?"

"An S.P. came to get him. Took him up to the captain's quarters," he responded with a stern face.

Oh. I asked cautiously, "Lee, too?"

"Took him away, too."

"Do you know what's going on?" I asked hesitantly.

"No idea," he answered with a black look, "but I hope bunking in Mr. Huang's cabin isn't going to get *me* in trouble."

I pouted my lips at him. "He's a very nice man."

"Maybe he is."

"And he was good to you."

He nodded. "I'm just glad to get off that damn ship."

"Where will you go now?" I asked in an effort to be polite to this surly young man.

His expression relaxed a bit. "San Francisco. I hear there's lots of Chinese there."

"Well, good luck."

"You, too," Dao-Zeun said, showing the tips of his teeth. As I returned to stand with my family in the lineup, a rotund Red Cross lady came along and gave us ham sandwiches and cold bottles of Coca-Cola, which Mother declined.

"Oh, my dear, you're not looking well," the woman said. "I'll bring you a cup of tea, would that do?"

"That would be lovely," Mother said gratefully, and within minutes the woman returned with cups of tea for all of us.

At a long table nearby, a Customs official was looking through various suitcases belonging to a middle-aged woman in a moth-eaten fur coat.

And then I noticed that a man and woman at some distance ahead of us were being escorted with their luggage into one of the side rooms with closed doors. A number of minutes went by before they came out again, looking very unhappy and being closely accompanied by the Customs official, who signaled to one of the S.P.s standing guard, and the policeman quickly stepped up and took the couple away. I guessed they had tried to smuggle something in and had been caught at it.

It made me think of the two gems Mrs. Dobson always carried with her in that little embroidered bag. Would the Customs men find those? No doubt they would, because her husband had charged her with stealing them. But Dad had told Captain Jackson that she'd taken them because they were all Lee and she had to live on. And now she would be hoping to find work in this country. What about that? Americans didn't like Germans right now. If the Immigration people let them in, would anyone hire this woman who was really Dr. von Sternberg?

Feeling heavy-hearted, I finished drinking my tea and volunteered to take our empty glass cups back to the Red Cross area, located not far from where we stood in line.

As I was returning, I saw that an S.P. was talking with my father!

I hurried up anxiously, and Dad said, "It's nothing to worry about, Janet. Captain Jackson wants to see us again, that's all."

He turned back to the S.P., a handsome young man with a deep tan and soft lights in his steel-blue eyes. "What about our loads, then?" Dad asked. "Who will see them through Customs?"

The S.P. waved to a Customs man, who sauntered

up, looking bored. He was lean and ferret-faced, with dark unruly hair that needed a shampoo. He inspected our family passport and consulted his clipboard.

"Baylor. Medical missionaries. Two steamers, two trunks, five crates. Kashmiri tables, rugs, that sort of thing, I suppose. No problem, we'll take care of it."

Hugh touched the man's arm and said with a concerned look, "It's not just tables and rugs, my collections of stamps and bugs are in there, too, so be careful when you handle those."

Hugh and his bugs and stamps! I thought impatiently. It seemed to me sometimes he loved them more than anything. When we would be at home on vacation in Taxila, he would spend hours and hours sorting out his carefully preserved collection of bugs and beetles — specimens that included little blue bugs as bright as sapphires, tiny green ones that looked like emeralds, the two-inch black rhinoceros beetles with their fierce-looking pincers, and four perfect (and rare) brown elephant beetles, as big as the palm of my hand. And his stamps — how I hated those stamps when I wanted him to come out and play with me! I could see they were pretty, yes, all those special diamond-shaped ones from Tibet and Burma, and the old ones in triangles from Siam. But, compared to the outdoors, stamps seemed dull to me, and only because Hugh also loved roaming the fields and climbing the trees near our house was I usually able to coax him away from his albums.

My reverie of those days in Taxila was interrupted by

the Customs man who was saying laconically to Hugh, "We'll take good care of it, kid. Bugs and stamps, you say? We'll see to it, don't you worry."

"All right, then, Dr. Baylor," the S.P. said, "I'll escort you and your family to Captain Jackson's quarters."

The Customs man held up a hand. "First I want to check the doctor's briefcase and medical bag. And the kid's koala."

"My koala!" I exclaimed.

"For goodness sake . . . !" Mother began.

"No fear, ladies. Routine check. Won't take a sec," he said as he took the koala from me, ran his hand carefully up and down its back and stomach and sides, pinched its ears, and handed it back to me. "You see, no problem."

Hugh asked with interest, "What were you expecting to find, Sir?"

"Sometimes we find that kids' stuffed animals make great hiding places for things their parents don't want to pay duty on, so I look for a seam that hadn't ought to be there."

He pointed to Dad's medical bag. "Open it up."

"Is that entirely necessary?" Dad objected. "There's just the ordinary pills and injectables and a few instruments . . ."

"Open it," the man commanded.

Dad scowled. He seemed ready to make a further objection but clenched his jaw as he pulled the key chain from his pocket. He released the metal clasps and carefully laid the two halves of the bag open to expose the neat rows of bottles and the side pockets so impeccably packed.

"Take it all out," the man ordered.

"No, I don't want to do that," Dad said stubbornly. "I see no need for that. Are you the chief agent here?"

The man shook his head.

"Let me talk to your supervisor, then."

"Take it easy, Doc. I was just wondering about morphine."

"A ridiculous concern, if you ask me," Dad snapped. I saw that his face was flushed with angry impatience. "Why does everyone assume doctors carry massive supplies of morphine around with them? I have *some,* yes . . ." and using the four fingers of his right hand, he slid three little vials up out of their leather waistbands. "Here it is, see? That's it. And I also have a complete list of the bag's contents," he went on, patting his briefcase, "if you're interested."

"Okay, okay, Doc. You can close it. Just papers in the briefcase?"

"Just papers."

"That's all right, then," the man said with a nod to the S.P. "They can go."

We followed the S.P. up the gangplank, across the deck, up three narrow ladders, and then along the gangway that led to Captain Jackson's cabin where I'd had my birthday party.

The S.P. knocked and the door was opened by the captain himself, who motioned for us to stand aside while two men in gray flannel suits and black hats came out. They were carrying briefcases and had stern, self-important looks on their faces.

And then across the room I saw Lee! Sitting next to her mother! They were on a couch under an open porthole through which the sun glinted down on their two heads, brownish-black and blond, but their faces were in shadow, so I couldn't see whether they were happy or not. Mr. Huang was on a chair near them. And leaning against the wall behind Mr. Huang was a middle-aged, balding man with thick glasses and a pursed mouth. He wore an expensive-looking blue pin-striped suit with a blue tie that had little white sailboats all over it. I saw that his expression instantly brightened with expectation as he regarded my father.

Quickly crossing the room, I sat on the carpet at Lee's feet and looked up at her. "What's happening?" I whispered.

"Things are working out," she said, her dark eyes shining. "Those men you just saw were from an important office."

Mrs. Dobson leaned down and said quietly, "The Department of Justice. Immigration." Although there was a sparkle in her eyes, her face looked pale and drawn, much as my mother's did after she'd recovered from a siege with a migraine headache.

Mrs. Dobson beckoned to my mother to sit beside her. Dad and my brothers seated themselves on the second couch, while the captain took the chair at his desk. The man in the blue suit remained standing.

The captain cleared his throat and said, "It's at Dr. von Sternberg's request that you're here. I'll let her say it." He gave her a nod.

"You will be pleased, I think," she began in a soft voice, "pleased to learn that, after one or two more formalities, Lily and I will probably be free to enter your country."

"Goodie!" I exclaimed along with the "Hurray!" and "Thank goodness!" and "Oh, I'm so pleased!" from the others.

"What sort of formalities?" Dad asked.

"She'll need to appear in court, for one thing," the captain said. "We've obtained counsel for her," he added with a nod in the direction of the man who was leaning against the wall. "Mr. Amos Meyer has agreed to be her attorney. Do you want to say anything at this point, Mr. Meyer?"

"Not much," the man replied with a frown, "except to say I am quite confident we can clear up the charges against her and restore her good name. She understands, of course, that she'll be on probation and under surveillance for the duration of the war. Under the circumstances of her present situation, however, the men who were just here determined it would be unjust to deny her and her daughter legal entry."

"You see, Jannie?" Kevin said with a happy smile. "I *told* you it was a good country!"

Mrs. Dobson looked down at her hands. "They say I need someone to sponsor me. I thought perhaps . . ."

"She'd like you to sponsor her, Dr. Baylor," the captain put in.

"Sponsor?" Dad asked. "What exactly does that entail? At the moment I'm without work myself, you understand. I'd be in no position to hire her, much as I . . ."

"No, no, nothing like that," the captain interrupted. "You need simply to attest to her good character and the likelihood of her being able to work to support herself and her child."

"That I can certainly do," Dad said firmly. "As to where she would find work, well . . ."

"She'll be obliged to stay in California for a time."

"I see." Dad rubbed his chin that was beginning to show a five-o'clock shadow. He gave her an encouraging nod. "I did my internship at Los Angeles County General Hospital. A very busy place. I would try there first, if I were you. I trust you have your medical diploma and other papers of certification and recommendation with you?"

"From the University of Heidelberg, yes."

"An excellent university, I know, but not well regarded at present," Dad said with a hint of apology.

"You must be prepared to work at a level no higher than that of a nurse's aide, perhaps, until such time as you've passed the medical examinations required by the state. And, as a foreigner, you will be asked to take a comprehensive examination in English which, in your case, should pose no problem.

"But the very *first* thing you must do," he went on with an urgent nod, "is to apply for citizenship, so that, in seeking employment, you can demonstrate you're in the process of becoming a United States citizen. I assume both you and your daughter hope to become U.S. citizens?"

They both smiled and nodded.

Captain Jackson glanced at the lawyer and said, "Mr. Meyer is prepared to help them with that."

The captain then suggested that when the German doctor applied for her citizenship papers, she might want to drop the "von" from her name.

"I've traced the name von Sternberg back eleven generations!" she objected. "I'm very proud of my name."

"Aristocracy and all that, I suppose," Captain Jackson said with a dismissive grunt.

Once again Kevin looked across the room at me and said, "In our country we don't talk about that sort of thing."

"I *know* that," I said, feeling resentful that he was giving me these lessons in public. "Miss Henshaw said for us it's only money that counts."

"Not true!" Dad exclaimed in amazement. He gave the captain a quick, apologetic smile. "Miss Henshaw was her teacher in boarding school. A young English woman."

"That explains it," Captain Jackson said with a grimace. "The English have always presumed to know more about us than we do."

He turned back to Mrs. Dobson and said with a cynical glint in his eyes, "You might want to keep the name that's on your passport."

"I wouldn't want to do that," she responded quietly.

Captain Jackson shrugged. "Suit yourself. But I would make things easier on yourself, if I were you."

He got up from his desk and went to the copper table I'd noticed on the day of my party. The glass decanters on it were filled at different levels with clear and amber-colored liquids, and he touched each of their stoppers, as though trying to decide which one to select. Then he looked at my father.

"I don't suppose you'd like a drink?"

"Liquor?" Dad asked sharply. "No *thank* you!"

"Missionaries. I might have guessed. Teetotalers, no doubt."

"Yes," Dad said stiffly, as though he'd just sat on a pineapple.

Mother smiled uncertainly and glanced at Mrs. Dobson, Mr. Huang, and Mr. Meyer. "But perhaps the others . . . ?"

Mr. Meyer shook his head.

"Mr. Huang doesn't drink either," Mrs. Dobson said.

"But *you* do," I said quickly. "Go ahead! Don't mind us!"

Dad scowled at me. I raised my eyebrows at him. I hated it when he was stuffy like that, so holier-than-thou, although he didn't like it when *I* acted that way. And it also made me mad the way the captain had asked only Dad, as though the rest of us weren't in the room.

I think the captain got my message, because he colored a bit and said under his breath, "It might be better if I just order up coffee and so on for everyone."

He did so, and after a steward had brought in a tray of coffee and sandwiches, and we'd all helped ourselves, the captain said, "Well then, Doctor, all we need is your signature on this attestation."

Kevin leaned over the plate on his lap. "Captain, I guess you now know Mr. Patel is really a Chinese man named Pogogh Chang. Is that guy going to get off scot-free after having caused all this trouble?"

Mr. Meyer, the lawyer, wagged a thin finger at him. "We can't discuss those issues at the present moment, young man."

"Well, uh, you need to look into his bank account and see how much money he got from Mrs. Dobson."

Mr. Meyer's lips twitched in the hint of a smile. "It's the first thing on my agenda."

I asked Mrs. Dobson, "So what's gonna happen next?"

Mr. Meyer answered for her: "While Dr. von Sternberg is waiting for her court appearance, we'll put her and her daughter up in a local hotel. When it's over, they can contact you to let you know how things went."

Kevin smoothed his napkin and began writing on it. "This is our grandparents' address in Grand Rapids. Write to us there." He handed it to Lee.

Then, as though someone had given a signal, we all stood and began shaking hands and saying goodbye.

I shook Mr. Huang's cool, dry hand and asked, "Where will you go?"

He gave me his sweet smile. "I stay with them. When it be over, maybe I also stay in City of Angels."

"I'm glad they have such a good friend," I said before turning to give Mrs. Dobson a big hug. "Write as soon as you can! We'll all be dying to know what happens to you."

"Lily and I will both write," she said, giving me a kiss on the cheek. "You're a good friend, too. Your whole family's wonderful."

I hugged Lee and said, "I think you're beautiful. I didn't want to tell you that, but you *are*. And don't you worry, you'll do fine in school."

She kissed the tip of my nose. "Thanks. I would have gone crazy without you."

247

I watched her go over to Hugh. The two of them shook hands like they were about thirty years old and had only just met.

Next she held out a hand to Kevin, but he said, "Come on, give me a hug!" and when they'd finished, Hugh said shyly, "Well, then, I guess I get one, too," and he squeezed her so hard she squealed.

We finally got out of there.

On the deck the air was clear and brisk. The last of an orange sun was melding with the far steely line of the Pacific as we took our final walk down the gangplank. On shore, a few pale lights had come on.

Dad first phoned the Van Andels and then made arrangements with the Customs Chief for our extra luggage and crates to be delivered to the train station and kept in storage for the next week, until we left for the Midwest.

The Van Andels arrived in an enormous shiny blue car called a DeSoto, with flaps that could go over its headlights, like eyelids. The woman looked amazingly huge in her fur coat, but I liked her white smile and her brown eyes that sparked with warmth and energy. She looked as though she'd never known a sick day in her life. Her husband, too, was robust and cheerful, hefting our two steamers into the trunk of the car with a little help from Kevin.

And off we went, driving down avenues that were dark now except for a few yellow streetlamps. To the left and right of us I could make out neatly trimmed lawns and bushes and a few white fences, beyond which the fine houses' windows were curtained, and I wondered what was going on in all of those private rooms.

"It all looks so clean," Mother said quietly.

I saw Mr. Van Andel glance at his wife, but neither of them said anything, and we drove on in silence for a while, until we passed through an open gate and drove up a long gravel driveway lined with palm trees. Ahead was a one-story, sprawling house that reminded me a bit of our bungalow in Taxila, except that this house was far more grand and it seemed they'd left a light on in every single room.

"Here we are!" Mr. Van Andel said.

We kids spent the next half-hour exploring the house — room after carpeted room of furniture in leather or plush upholstery, with hibiscus and other plants growing indoors; rooms with big beds covered with thick bedspreads and heaped with matching pillows; bathrooms with blue basins and toilets and sparkling fixtures; a kitchen with slick yellow countertops and shiny taps extending over a large white sink, and, in one corner, a refrigerator! We'd seen refrigerators and freezers on board ship, but we'd never imagined ordinary people had them. During all of our years in Taxila, we'd kept things cool in an icebox. The ice came in a burlap-wrapped twenty-pound block each morning on the train from Rawalpindi, and our cook brought it to the house on the back of his bicycle.

"They must be rich," Hugh whispered in my ear.

The next morning we discovered the heated swimming pool. We swam and played in it until Mr. Van Andel coaxed us out with the hamburgers he'd made on his outdoor grill. The following day we spent an entire afternoon at the billiard table in the basement recreation room. And every day Mrs. Van Andel baked a new treat of some sort. Butter and sugar were rationed, she said, but she'd been saving them up for our arrival. They treated us like royalty.

One day our whole family went with them to help shop for groceries, followed by a trip to a big department store. Strange to say, that excursion was not as pleasant as we had thought it would be; in fact it made us irritable. The spectacle of such a vast variety of things on display was overwhelming. And so many different *kinds* of each thing — such as cold cereal, jam, peanut butter, and dog food! It was too much for us. America was at war, but we would never have guessed it, to look at all the goods that were available. The Van Andels, however, complained a good deal about the shortage of things. We began to feel we'd come from a different planet.

We were all very quiet at supper — another huge spread.

Mr. Van Andel wanted to know what we thought of the department store.

"I liked the escalators," Hugh said.

The man's big chest rumbled with a chuckle. "A newfangled thing to you, eh? Not many stores in the

States have them yet, but they'll catch on. More economical than elevators, they say, and better for business, because as you're going along you see things you might like to buy."

"I don't remember seeing much," Hugh said. "Jannie and I just liked running up the ones that were going down and down the ones going up. Until a guy in a uniform told us to cut it out."

Mr. Van Andel shook his head at us. "You'll get used to it. By the time you're my age, you won't remember you ever did that, they'll be so common."

Mother said quietly, "I doubt that any of us will forget this week; you've been so good to us."

Later, when our family was alone together, we worried about what we could give the Van Andels as a token of our gratitude for their generosity.

"We'll send them one of our Persian rugs," Mother said.

"They don't need a rug," Kevin said. "Everything's carpeted. Anyway, a rug would be too much. They'd be embarrassed because they did a lot for us but not *that* much."

"Let's send them one of our brass and copper vases," Hugh suggested. "Not everyone has a vase from India. And Mrs. Van Andel likes flowers."

So it was agreed an Indian vase would be a nice Thank You, and we went to bed feeling happy that we could give them something they didn't already have.

# Fifteen

I soon discovered that a week with the Van Andels as an introduction to the United States had been unrealistic. Not everyone was as wealthy as they were. In fact, as our train pulled into station after station on our journey to the Midwest, we saw pockets of severe poverty, with people living in mere shacks not far from the railroad tracks.

Dad said somewhat apologetically, "You're not getting to see the best of what these cities have to offer."

Mother nodded. "Railway stations are notoriously the worst part of town. I wonder why that has to be."

"Someday we'll drive across the country," Dad said. "That will be better."

But there were aspects of traveling by train that were fun. It was possible, for instance, to walk from car to car along the entire length of the train, and Hugh and I did it a number of times a day, until people got to know us and either smiled or frowned to see us coming again. In between times we sat a lot, of course, and played Old Maid and Monopoly.

And for hours and hours of those three days, we gazed out of the window. What impressed me the most, having come from crowded India, were the wide open spaces without a soul in sight.

The monotony was broken by mealtimes in the dining car, which I found elegant, with real linen napkins, little crystal vases full of petunias, and waiters in red uniforms.

But the best part of traveling Pullman, as Mike Turner had suggested, was at night when the steward came to pull down the beds from their hidden compartments. Kevin, Hugh, and I each had an upper one. Going up a little ladder to get to it was no different from Hugh's and Dad's upper bunks on the ship, but what made this bed special was that, once inside, there was a heavy curtain to be pulled shut, making the place cozy and private. And each bed had its own little window. I liked lying up there, looking out at the big sky, bright with stars, and sometimes seeing the lights of a town in the distance and wondering what it was like to be a rancher or a farmer or a factory worker. The clackety-clack of the wheels on the tracks had a lulling effect, as did the gentle sway of the train, rocking me to sleep.

We changed trains in Chicago and traveled the final hours through a snowstorm. I sat at a window for a long time. It was new to me to see a world outside that was covered in white, the air dense with fast-falling flakes.

At last we pulled into the station of Grand Rapids, Michigan, and there on the platform was a group of about thirty people, waving to us. Relatives.

"There's Mother!" my mother said happily.

My maternal grandma was a plump little woman with a round face and light blue eyes. She had a knitted cap pulled down over her ears and wore a shabby-looking green coat that hung to the tops of her laced-up black boots. When I got up close to her, I saw in her expression a certain gentleness but also a no-nonsense stolidness that made me think here was a woman who rarely felt sorry for herself. I loved her immediately, even before she put her arms around me and kissed my ear. The soft skin of her neck smelled faintly of vanilla.

My maternal grandfather was a tall, broad-shouldered, taciturn man who didn't hug us and didn't take off his woolen glove when he shook hands. I could see it was going to be hard to warm up to him.

But my father's father, whom we kids called Grandpa, was lovable. He'd lived alone ever since my grandmother had died before I was born. I watched him clasp my father to him with great energy; there were tears in his sunken blue eyes. His stooped shoulders made him shorter than Dad. His gray coat was frayed at the collar and cuffs, his heavy black shoes badly scuffed. He gave me a bearhug, his whiskered

chin prickling my cheek. His clothing smelled of to-
bacco smoke.

Then there were various aunts and uncles and
cousins from both sides of the family who came up to
greet me and exclaimed over how much I'd grown in
the past seven years, as though that were an unusual
phenomenon. I felt shy at first, meeting so many
strangers, but the interesting thing about relatives is
that you don't feel strange with them for very long. I
could see certain features of my immediate family repeated in their faces, and there was a warmth in their
expressions that was quite different from the polite
smiles of mere new acquaintances.

It was cold and snowy on the station platform. As
soon as possible, everyone went into the waiting room,
where it was decided a number of get-togethers would
occur later in the week; but for the time being our family was to go to Grandma's house, and Grandpa Baylor,
who had never learned to drive, came with us in my
other grandfather's old Ford.

Mother had told me her parents had lived in the
same house all of their fifty-five years of marriage and
Grandma had borne all ten of her children there, two of
whom had died in infancy of diphtheria. I was eager to
see the house, and when we finally turned a corner onto
Kalamazoo Avenue, Mother leaned forward and
pointed, "There!"

It was an ordinary two-story wooden house painted

yellow with white trimming around the windows. A fresh inch of snow lay on the walkway that Grandfather had obviously shoveled before leaving for the station because everywhere else the snow was two feet deep.

Inside, the house smelled of soap and freshly baked bread. The rooms were small and humbly furnished. A few faded rugs were spread here and there on the bare wood floors.

Everyone headed straight for the kitchen, which was perhaps the most spacious room in the house and wonderfully warm from the heat of an enormous black woodstove in one corner. Crisp white curtains were pulled back from the window that looked out on snow-covered branches of trees that Grandma said were peach and apple and pear, and wouldn't we have a good time canning the fruit next summer! The kitchen floor was covered with blue linoleum in a pattern of yellow triangles that had disappeared in the places where people had walked the most.

We drew chairs up to the big oak table in the middle of the kitchen. Grandma poked around in the coals of the stove, shoved a big piece of wood in, and put a pot of coffee on. Grandpa Baylor made little sounds of contentment as he lit his pipe and watched Mother slice a loaf of brown bread. She put a large wedge of Dutch spiced cheese on the table.

The Van Andels had served us the same cheese, I recalled, but there was no comparison in any other regard: Their grand house had filled me with awe, it's true, but instinctively I felt that this place was *home*.

We slept upstairs in unheated bedrooms — Mother and Dad in one, Hugh and I in another. Kevin, removed from us once again, had a bed in the attic. It was cold. But Grandma had given us lots of blankets.

In the morning, Hugh and I grabbed our clothes and raced downstairs. Grandfather had a fire going in a pot-bellied stove in the living room, where we dressed before going into Grandma's warm kitchen. She'd made oatmeal. We ate it with milk and brown sugar. It tasted good.

Midmorning, while I was helping Grandma shell walnuts for a cake, and Mother was in the basement doing some laundry on Grandma's scrub board, our trunks and crates arrived from the train station. Dad and Kevin and Hugh went out to store them in the garage until we had a house of our own.

When my dad and brothers didn't come back into the house for what seemed like a long time, I went out to see what was going on.

Hugh was sitting on the garage floor, crying bitterly. Dad and Kevin were squatting on either side of him, comforting him.

"Someone's taken all his best stamps and best bugs," Kevin informed me.

"But how . . . who?"

"It must have been a Customs agent," Dad said heavily. He pointed to an open album, its two middle pages full of holes. "All his Burmese and Siamese diamonds and triangles. Cut them right out with a very sharp knife. Knew exactly which ones were valuable.

"And look here," he went on, indicating one of the shallow felt-bottomed and glass-covered boxes in which Hugh had carefully pinned down and labeled, in both English and Latin, each of his treasured specimens of bugs and beetles. "Took all four of his elephant beetles and the two best rhinoceros beetles."

I knelt down beside Hugh and put my arms around him. I felt heartsick for him. How many hundreds of hours he'd put into these fine collections! And someone, on seeing his careful work, instead of admiring it, had stolen it, and in doing so had violated a personal, private part of Hugh's mind. I understood that in that moment because of Hugh's crying, such as I'd never witnessed before. Sure, in boarding school, when we would meet for a few minutes every day at lunchtime, I'd sometimes seen his eyes get a bit red with suppressed tears when he'd had a bad time with the bullies or with his boarding master, but I'd never seen him actually cry. This thing that someone had done to him wasn't a physical hurt; it was more serious than that.

"I thought Customs agents worked for the United

States government," I said angrily to Dad. "They all had uniforms on."

"Yes, they're government employees," Dad replied, "but a uniform does not confer moral rectitude."

"What does *that* mean?" I asked irritably.

"It means," Kevin said, "that you can't trust a person just 'cause he's got a uniform on. They're still the same person underneath."

"Can't we find who did this and get him punished for it?" I asked.

"I'll certainly try," Dad said firmly. "I'm going to take photos of the album pages and of the boxes that show specimens missing. I'll send them along with a letter of complaint straight to Washington."

With a hopeful glint in his eyes, Hugh looked up at Dad, who said quickly, "I doubt anything will come of it, Hugh."

"Why not?"

"It's going to be impossible to prove. Furthermore, the people in Washington have far greater concerns on their minds these days, I'm afraid."

I said sullenly, "You told me America was the best country in the world."

"I believe it is, Janet. But no one said it was perfect."

Hugh stood, picked up his stamp albums and boxes of bugs and beetles, and walked with them very deliberately to the barrel in the backyard where Grandfather burned the trash.

"Hugh!" I yelled. "Don't throw them away!"

He turned his pale, thin face to me. "You want 'em? I sure don't."

"But Dad's gotta take those pictures first!"

"Never mind."

He chucked them all away.

A week later, a fat envelope arrived from California. In it were letters from Anna von Sternberg and Lily.

The first letter began:

*Dear Friends,*

*I hope you arrived with joy in your hometown. Lily and I miss you so much. Often in these past days we have wished we could talk with you. Mr. Huang has been a great support and comfort to us, but still we, all three of us, feel strange and lonely here at times.*

*The Court proceedings, once they began, did not take very long, and you will be pleased to know the Court has cleared us for residence in the United States, given certain restrictions because I am German. I understand that, and can only say I am grateful Judge Wurzburg does not consider every German a Nazi.*

*At your suggestion, Doctor Baylor, I have made contact with Los Angeles General Hospital and have an interview scheduled for next Tuesday. Judge Wurzburg says he will send along an affidavit for me. People have been kind to us.*

*No doubt it will take time for our hearts and minds to acquire a measure of peace here, but I must say I already feel tremendously relieved to know that Pogogh Chang is no longer a threat to us.*

*Thank you so much for your support and for your faith in me.*

*Best regards,*
*Anna*

"Oh, I'm so pleased!" Mother exclaimed. "Now let's see what Lily has to say."

Lily's letter was less formal. It read:

*Hi, so what's up?*

*It's been pretty dull here stuck in this hotel. I hope we can move to an apartment soon all our own. I like listening to the radio. Have you heard Tom Mix? And the Lone Ranger? Also Terry and the Pirates. On Sunday is the best, called the Shadow. Mother makes me do math problems to get ready for school. Sometimes Mr. H plays chess with me. I love potato chips. One day we went shopping. I got eleven new things — all clothes stuff but nice, and got my hair cut. I miss you. Write soon.* *Love, Lily*

*P.S. hugs and kisses OOOOOXXXXX*
*See, one for each of you.*

That evening I wrote the following letter:

Dear Lee,

Got your letter. Thanks. Glad things are working out for you and your mom. I miss you too.

My grandma is so nice I wish you could meet her. I like the house we're in but the bedrooms are cold. It snows a lot here.

We've been listening to the radio too, mostly stuff about the war. My dad keeps a map with colored pins stuck all over it and he moves them back and forth up by Poland and along the coast of France, down in Italy, over in Burma, all over the place. Makes me think of watching Mr. H and Dao-Zeun playing chess. I listen specially to what's going on in the Pacific islands since we were near there. Last night we heard the Japs have lost 300 planes and 500 ships out there and Hugh and I cheered but Mother told us to stop it since it meant lots of lives even though they weren't on our side. It's hard to know what to think except I want us to win. Dad says it looks like it won't be over soon so now Kevin's worried he'll have to go, he wants to be in the Navy.

I hope you and your mom and Mr. H can come visit us sometime. Have you heard the new song — Marezeedotes and doeszeedotes and little lambszeeivee? If you don't know what it means I'll tell you next time.

Write again as soon as you can. Lots of love to you and your mom. And hi to Mr. Huang.

Janet

*P.S. Send me a picture of you with your new haircut.*
*P.P.S. Hugh and Kevin send their love. My parents*
*too. My mom is writing your mom.*

In church on Sunday, the pastor read out the names of two young men from Grand Rapids who had perished at sea that week. The news made everyone very subdued. The organist played a few strains and we all stood up to sing in quavering voices that gradually grew stronger:

> *Eternal Father, strong to save,*
> *Whose arm doth bind the restless wave;*
> *Who bidd'st the mighty ocean deep*
> *Its own appointed limits keep;*
> *O, hear us when we cry to Thee*
> *For those in peril on the sea.*

But it isn't just the ocean itself that is sometimes perilous, I thought; it is people in other ships, people who are enemies. I noticed the date of the hymn: 1860. That was back in the days when men went to sea in sailing ships, back in the days before there were torpedoes from underneath and bombs from above. But even then, I recalled from my reading, there was always the risk of encountering pirates. Heck, seafarers since the times of Homer and St. Paul knew it was *people* you really needed to worry about.

In the car on the way home from church, I said, "It's people more than anything else that make other people cry, isn't it?"

Mother gave me a searching look. "More than fires and floods and tornadoes? That sort of thing, you mean?"

Although I hadn't thought of all those things, I nodded. Yes, that's what I'd meant: people, rather than those kinds of natural disasters.

"You may be right," Mother said softly. "People find they can do without *things*, but when they lose a person dear to their hearts . . . or when another person has hurt them, it's much harder."

After a few moments she went on, "But don't forget, it's people, also, who bring us our very best moments in life."

"How true!" Dad said heartily. "Please, kids, don't let this war make you cynical."

"Meaning what?" I snapped.

"Well, sounds to me like you've already lost your innocence," he replied evenly. "Which isn't all bad, mind you. But just don't close your heart up. Remember to keep a door open for good surprises."

Before I went to sleep that night, I watched the snow blow in onto my heavy layer of blankets. (Hugh and I always left the window open a crack. It was freezing in the room anyway, and we both liked the fresh air.) I thought about what Mother and Dad had said. And I thought about the fact that tomorrow we kids were going to have our first day at school. What will the other kids be like? I wondered. And what will our teachers be like? Some would be okay, I guessed, and some wouldn't be. Dad had warned us not to talk about India much nor about our voyage at sea. Our new acquaintances would be cautious about making friends with us if they discovered we'd had adventures they knew nothing about. We should simply do our best to try to fit in, he'd said.

Ho hum, I thought, I *like* being different. I would try to fit in, sure, but fit in as *me,* not by pretending to be just like everyone else.

Hugh rolled over in his bed next to mine. "You awake?"

"Yup."

"Whatcha thinkin' about?"

"Whether or not I'm going to like school tomorrow."

"Sure you will. You *like* school."

"But . . ."

"And you like *life,* Jannie," he added encouragingly. "Heck, it's basically no different here than anywhere else."

"What do you mean!" I protested. "It's *very* different here!"

"In *good* ways, mainly, so far, don't you think?"

"You can say that, even though your stamps . . . ?"

"Heck, that was just one bad guy," Hugh said quietly into the darkness. "I'm not saying there aren't others, you know, but . . . Look, we'll talk again tomorrow night, okay? We'll see how we feel then."

"Okay," I said, rolling over onto my right side and pulling the covers up over my ear, "we'll see."

## THE END

# Author's note

On January 1, 1944, a troopship, dubbed the *U.S.S. You Know Who*, began its journey from Bombay, India, to San Pedro, California, via Melbourne and Bora Bora, arriving safely on February 8, 1944.

I was a child then, traveling on that troopship with my family after having lived in India for seven years. Our journey across the Indian and Pacific oceans — when World War II was at its height in that region — was hazardous. There were, indeed, a number of frightening times, as described here. In general, however, we found the voyage interesting and memorable.

But memory is unreliable, and so this novel is also the product of my imagination. The members of the Baylor family resemble those of my own family as we were then, but all of the other characters, including Captain Jackson, are fictional.

I needed to do some research, too. At the time I began writing this book, I was living in Washington, D.C. I knew the real name of the ship and of her captain, and went with that information to the National Archives where I hoped to find the captain's log. Much to my disappointment, a Navy consultant told me the logs of troopship deployment during World War II ultimately fell under the jurisdiction of the Army and all such records were destroyed. He suggested that I go to the Office of Naval Records and Library where I would find the captain's War Diary.

In the Naval Library I found a listing of the troopship's various trips. On being admitted to the top floor of Naval Records, I was presented with three boxes of the captain's War Diary. I read only the dated pages that were of interest to me, each of which was marked CONFIDENTIAL and counter-stamped DECLASSIFIED. Much of the information was dry stuff, such as:

1030 All engines ahead standard 16.0 knots, departed Bora Bora, set course 021° true.

1045 Adjusted course to 026° true.

But I did find mention of a civilian death on board, of the fires, and of the sightings of other ships. The fact that hundreds of wounded troop-class passengers had embarked at Melbourne, however, was not documented in those terms. Nor was the fact that one stormy night the ship had come perilously close to tipping over. Given the captain's first note of 1/1/44, which reads, "Steaming singly . . . Zig-zagging during daylight and moonlight, when visibility and weather conditions permit," I wondered if he'd been too embarrassed to record the incident, so I called my consultant at the National Archives. "Yes," he said with a laugh, "I think he wouldn't have wanted to put down that the swells caught him between a zig and a zag." I still wonder, though, if the captain confided such concerns in his log.

My sincere thanks to the men and women, members of the U.S. Navy, who evinced interest in my project, gave me direction, and provided me with access to the material I was keen on reading.

JBM